The Little People

The Little People

STORIES OF FAIRIES, PIXIES, AND OTHER SMALL FOLK

Neil Philip

HARRY N. ABRAMS, INC.
NEW YORK

FOR JANICE SHAY

Library of Congress Cataloging-in-Publication Data

Philip, Neil.
    The little people : stories of fairies, pixies, and other small folk / by Neil Philip.
        p. cm.
Summary: Describes the origins, physical characteristics, dwelling places, activities, and special powers of different types of fairy folk from around the world. Illustrative traditional stories from various cultures are interspersed throughout the text.
    ISBN 0-8109-0570-1
1. Fairies. 2. Folklore. [1, Fairies. 2, Folklore.] I. Title.
GR549.P45 2002
398.21–dc21

                        2001056739

An Albion Book
Conceived, designed, and produced by The Albion Press Ltd.,
Spring Hill, Idbury, Oxon OX7 6RU, UK

Designed by Emma Bradford
Line illustrations by Jacqueline Mair
The text is set in 14/18-point Weiss, with hand-lettered headings.
Text copyright © 2002 by Neil Philip
Line illustrations copyright © 2002 by Jacqueline Mair
For details of color illustrations and their sources, see p.111.

Published in 2002 by Harry N. Abrams, Incorporated, New York
All rights reserved. No part of the contents of this book may be reproduced without the written consent of the publisher.

Typesetting by YHT, London
Color origination by Classic Scan, Singapore
Printed and bound in Hong Kong/China by South China Printing Company

10 9 8 7 6 5 4 3 2 1

Harry N. Abrams, Inc.
100 Fifth Avenue
New York, N.Y. 10011
www.abramsbooks.com

Abrams is a subsidiary of

LA MARTINIÈRE
G R O U P E

Contents

The World of the Fairies

THE WORLD OF the fairies has long been believed to overlap our world in some mysterious way. Time is not the same in the fairy world, and a night spent at fairy revels may be a year in human terms. Though we dwell on the same earth, we do not live in the same physical world. What looks like a grass-covered hill to us may be a palace of the fairies.

Fairies, it is said, can cast a "glamour" over humans, making us see things that are not truly there. A glamour is a spell or enchantment; even in the word's modern use, when we say that someone is glamorous, we suggest that there is something not quite real about his or her beauty. But we are still magnetically attracted to it—and the same is true of the beauty of the fairy world.

When human beings get a glimpse of the fairies, they are often left hungering to know more. To one who has been touched by fairy glamour, our everyday world seems dull. Our food has no savor, our laughter rings hollow. It is the fairy world, the Perilous Realm, for which the person longs.

The realm of the fairies is perilous because the nature of the fairies themselves is unpredictable. Sometimes they are friendly, sometimes hostile. Sometimes helpful, sometimes deceitful. Sometimes good, but often mischievous and sometimes downright wicked. Often generous, but always quick to anger.

1

By fairies I mean all kinds of magical beings who can take a human or semihuman form, whether they are the winged fairies of the air, the solitary fairies such as the household hob or the leprechaun, the underground dwellers such as dwarfs and gnomes, the freshwater fairies such as kelpies, or the saltwater fairies such as mermaids and selkies. The fairy folk are as diverse as we are, and range from majestic elves to malevolent trolls.

The origin of the fairies is explained in various ways. Sometimes they are thought of as a separate race of beings, the People of Peace, who have always existed alongside human beings. Sometimes they are said to be an earlier race of beings, who have been supplanted by humans. Sometimes they are said to be the souls of the dead who are neither good enough for heaven nor wicked enough for hell.

In Ireland and Scotland fairies are often believed to be angels who were cast out of heaven after the rebellion of Lucifer. When God shut the doors of heaven and hell, all those who were in either place remained, but many were caught between, still falling through the air. Some fell on the land and some on the sea, and wherever they landed they became the fairy folk.

In Scandinavia the fairies are called the Hidden People, and they are believed to be descended from the children whom Eve hid from God, as this Icelandic story tells.

THE ORIGIN OF THE ELVES

Once God Almighty visited Adam and Eve. They were glad to see him, and made him welcome. They showed him around their house, which was sparkling clean; and he admired the children whom they called in to meet him.

"What fine children," God said. "Do you have any more?"

"No," said Eve, but that was a lie. The truth was that Eve had a number of other children; but they had not been washed, and she did not want God to see them when they were dirty. When she saw God coming, she had pushed them out of sight and told them to stay hidden.

God knew this, and said, "That which has been hidden from me shall be hidden from all."

So the children Eve concealed from God became the elves, who live in the woods and on the open moors, and in rocks and hills and caves, while the children she showed to God became the human beings.

Elves are invisible to human beings unless they wish to be seen. They are the Hidden People.

Some human beings encounter the Hidden People by accident, and others are sought out by them because the Hidden People need their help. Still others, such as the Irish poet W. B. Yeats, go

looking for them on purpose. Yeats was fascinated by the supernatural: by magic and astrology and visions. He particularly loved the idea of the fairies: "Nations of gay creatures, having no souls; nothing in their bright bodies but a mouthful of sweet air."

Yeats asked old Irish peasants about the fairies and found that they accepted them as a natural part of their world. One old Galway countryman, renowned as a seer and healer, told Yeats, "I see them in all places, and there's no man mowing a meadow that doesn't see them at some time or another."

More than anything else, Yeats longed to see a fairy for himself, and on October 14, 1892, he did.

THE POET AND THE FAIRY QUEEN

Yeats went walking along the sandy shore at Rosses Point in County Sligo, in northwestern Ireland. With him were his uncle, a middle-aged man, and his cousin, a young woman who like Yeats himself saw visions and who was said to have once narrowly escaped being made captive by the fairies.

They stopped at a cave that was a haunt of the fairies, the Forgetful People. Yeats made a circle on the sand and invoked the fairies. Soon his uncle heard voices like boys shouting and the sound of distant music. His cousin saw a bright light and heard music, talking, and the sound of cheering and stamping feet, all coming from the heart of the rock. Then she saw them, a host of little people dressed in red, dancing to a tune she did not know.

Yeats summoned the queen of the fairies to come to him, and she did. She was not small but had the appearance of "a beautiful tall woman," with gold ornaments and dark hair. When asked, she called the fairies out of the cave and drew them up in four bands. One band carried boughs of mountain ash in their hands; another wore necklaces made of serpents' scales.

Yeats questioned the fairy queen closely, but often she did not understand what he wanted to know. When he asked her if fairies were not "dramatizations of our moods," she answered that her people were "much like human beings, and do most of the things human beings do."

In the end the practical fairy queen lost patience with the airy-fairy poet. She wrote in the sand, "Be careful, and do not seek to know too much about us." Then she vanished, and the poet, his uncle, and his cousin, were left alone on the shore, shivering as a cold wind blew in from the sea.

The fairy queen's instruction to Yeats not to "seek to know too much" echoes the traditional belief that it was unlucky to meddle in the affairs of the fairies, or to talk loosely or disrespectfully about them. As one old woman told Yeats, "I always mind my own affairs, and they always mind theirs."

One man who did seek to know too much was the Scottish minister Robert Kirk. Kirk was born in 1644 and was a seventh son, and so had the power of second sight. He was fascinated by the fairies and wrote the first known book about them, *The Secret Commonwealth of Elves, Fauns, and Fairies*, in which he concluded that fairies are "of a middle nature betwixt man and angel" with "bodies of congealed air."

Kirk knew all kind of things about the fairies—even that they believe, "that nothing perisheth, but (as the sun and year) every thing goes in a circle, lesser or greater, and is renewed and refreshed in its revolutions." He is supposed to have paid a great price for his curiosity.

THE SECRET COMMONWEALTH

Shortly after he completed the manuscript of his book, the Reverend Robert Kirk took a walk in the evening air. He was only wearing a nightshirt.

When he did not come home, the rest of the household searched for him and found his lifeless body lying on top of a fairy hill, one of those fairy dwellings with which Kirk himself records that it is "impious and dangerous" to meddle. The body was carried home and buried next day in the minister's own churchyard.

But later Robert Kirk appeared to one of his relatives and gave him a message for his cousin, Graham of Duchray. Kirk said that he was not dead; he was a captive in fairyland. His wife was expecting a child when he died, and Kirk promised that he would appear again at the child's christening. When he did so, Graham was to throw his knife over Kirk's head, and this would free him from the fairies' power, as their enchantments can be broken with cold iron.

At the christening, as all the family sat down to celebrate, the wraith of Robert Kirk appeared among them. But Graham of Duchray was so startled that he forgot to throw his knife. The moment passed, the apparition faded away, and Robert Kirk was never seen again.

And in the parish of Aberfoyle they will show you to this day the fairy hill where he dwells, a captive of the fairies about whom he asked one question too many.

Not all fairies live beneath fairy hills. Some live in rocks, or caves, or in wells, pools, or streams, while others share the homes of human beings, whether farmhouse or castle. There are also fairies of wild places, such as the Scandinavian wood elves.

One Norwegian woodcutter told how he saw one of these wood elves with his own eyes. She is one of the fairies whose glamour only works from in front. If you see her from behind, you realize she is completely hollow. When one of these fairies tries to entice a man into her power, he must keep his wits about him and ask her to turn around, and then the spell will be broken. "In my young days," he said, "I saw the wood fairy with my own eyes. She had a red knitted jacket, a green bodice, and blue gown. She ran past me with her long yellow hair flying loose about her. She was pretty in the face, but behind she was as hollow as a baking-trough."

Fairies are also often associated with flowers, and the folklore of Cornwall, in England's Celtic southwest, tells of the beautiful flowering gardens of the Cornish fairies.

On the Lizard Peninsula at the very western tip of Cornwall, near to Lands End, is a finely balanced stone called Logan Rock. This is a fairy place, and before it was tipped from its balance by Lieutenant Goldsmith on April 8, 1824, sick infants who were rocked on it could be magically cured. Although the rock was set back in place, the charm was broken.

On the southwest side of Logan Rock, where the cliffs run down to the sea, are the gardens of the Small Folk—beautiful green spots on the rock, where feathery ferns and delicate cliff pinks grow. The fairies who tend these gardens are beautiful creatures who love to do good. But they do not like it when human beings meddle with them, and get angry if someone they have helped brags about it.

Though by day you can see no flowers in their gardens save the pinks, by the midsummer moonlight the gardens blossom with flowers of every color, more beautiful than any mortal garden. One Cornish fisherman described how they looked from the sea: "When I have been to sea close under the cliffs, of a fine summer's night, I have heard the sweetest of music, and seen hundreds of little lights moving about amongst what looked like flowers. Ay! and they were flowers, too, for you may smell the sweet scent far out at sea. Indeed, I have heard many of the old men say that they have smelt the sweet perfume, and heard the music from the fairy gardens of the Castle, when more than a mile from the shore."

Once when a gang of smugglers were trying to land their contraband goods at Zennor, on the Lizard, they disturbed the fairies at their dancing. The little men were all dressed in green, with red caps. When a smuggler began to mock them, the Small Folk advanced with bows and arrows, spears and slings, looking fierce despite their size. The smuggler shouted, "Put to sea for your lives! There's thousands of small people and bucca-boos almost on our backs!" The smugglers had to abandon their goods and flee. They were safe on the sea, because the fairies could not abide saltwater.

Music and dance play a huge part in fairy life, but the fairies also, as the fairy queen told W. B. Yeats, do "most of the things human beings do." They hold markets and fairs, and they fall in and out of love. Scottish tradition records a fairy love song:

> I left in the doorway of the bower
> My jewel, the dusky, brown, white-skinned,
> Her eye like a star, her lip like a berry,
>   Her voice like a stringed instrument.
>
> I left yesterday in the meadow of the kine
> The brown-haired maid of sweetest kiss,
> Her eye like a star, her cheek like a rose,
>   Her kiss has the taste of pears.

It is above all the piercing "eye like a star" that shows that this is a fairy maiden, not a human girl.

Some, convinced that fairies are fallen angels, say that they can neither have children nor die, but remain always the same, unchanged and unchanging. But tradition tells of fairy children and of fairy funerals. Robert Kirk tells us that "they live much longer than we, yet die at last."

The poet William Blake was one of the few people who can claim to have seen a fairy funeral. In his garden, he said, he saw "a procession of creatures of the size and color of green and gray grasshoppers, bearing a body laid out on a rose-leaf, which they buried with songs, and then disappeared."

THE FUNERAL OF THE FAIRY QUEEN

One moonlit night a fisherman named Richard was returning home to Lelant in Cornwall. As he climbed the hill from St. Ives, he thought he heard the bell of Lelant Church tolling, and saw lights flickering in the windows. The bell was not clear and bright as usual, but muffled.

Curious, Richard walked up to the church and peered in through the window. At first he could see nothing; but then he saw a funeral procession. The central aisle was crowded with little people, who were wearing wreaths of wild roses and carrying boughs of blossoming myrtle.

Six of them were bearing a little coffin, and inside the coffin was a body about the size of a child's doll. The body was that of a beautiful woman, as lovely as an angel. It was covered in white flowers, and its golden hair was tangled among the blossoms.

10

Richard watched as a party of men with picks and spades dug a grave before the altar and then lowered the coffin into the hole. As they did so, they tore off their wreaths and broke their myrtle branches, crying, "Our queen is dead! Our queen is dead!"

When the grave was filled, the fairies began to wail and shriek, and Richard was so alarmed that he cried out too.

The lights went out and the fairies flew off. As they passed Richard, he felt the pinpricks as they thrust at him with tiny swords. He fled for his life.

For centuries it has been said that the fairies are dwindling and departing, chased away by the noise and confusion of we humans. One tradition records the final departure of the Scottish fairies.

THE DEPARTURE OF THE FAIRIES

One Sunday morning, in the little hamlet of Burn of Eathie, all the people had gone to church, save one herds-boy and his sister, who were lounging beside one of the cottages. Just as the shadow on the sundial touched noon, they saw a long cavalcade winding its way out of the woods and into the village.

The horses were shaggy little things, speckled dun and gray. The riders were stunted, ugly creatures, dressed in old-fashioned plaid jerkins, long gray cloaks, and little red caps. Their long hair was wild and uncombed.

The boy and his sister stood gazing in astonishment and dismay as rider after rider passed the cottage and disappeared into the brushwood on the hillside. At last only one rider, who was lagging behind the others, was left.

The boy plucked up his courage and asked, "What are you, little mannie?"

"Not of the race of Adam," said the creature.

"Where are you going?" asked the boy.

And then the little man turned in his saddle, looked the boy in the eye, and told him, "The People of Peace shall never more be seen in Scotland."

11

Fairy Folk

THERE ARE A bewildering number of different kinds of fairies. Some, often called the trooping fairies, live in societies rather like those of the humans around them; others live solitary lives, often attached to a particular place or a particular human family, or devoted to a particular occupation, such as the Irish leprechaun and his shoe-making.

This book is largely confined to the fairy folk of northern Europe, for the fairy lore of the Germanic, Scandinavian, and Celtic peoples is especially rich. However, the fairy kind are to be found all over the world. France has its naughty lutins; Italy, its folleti, who travel in knots of wind and control the weather; Russia, its forest spirits called leshiye. Some are helpful, such as the massariol of northern Italy, who is a jolly little fellow in a red hat, with a laugh like a horse and the face of an old man, who helps the farmers at their work. Others are best avoided, such as the vila of eastern Europe, a kind of female nature spirit with a vengeful and capricious nature.

In the west of England are to be found the pixies (sometimes spelled *pigsies* or *piskies*). These are mischievous but not malicious creatures who dress in green. They have red hair, pointed ears, snub noses, and squinty eyes. Their chief idea of fun is to mislead travelers, and someone who loses his or her way may have been "pixy led." The only way for the poor traveler to escape their spell is to turn his or her coat inside out.

Also in the West Country live the spriggans, little fairies who, like the korred of Brittany, an ancient Celtic kingdom in northern France, are associated with standing stones and buried treasure. A Cornish story tells how the lure of finding such treasure tempted one man to kidnap a spriggan child.

SKILLYWIDDEN

One day Uncle Billy was out on the hill, cutting furze. As he parted the furze with his cutting hook, he saw a pretty little creature asleep on a bank of wild thyme. It was a little man no bigger than a cat, dressed in a green coat, sky blue breeches and stockings, and diamond-buckled shoes, with a little three-cocked hat pulled over his face to shade it from the sun.

"It's a spriggan," said Uncle Billy. "If I can catch hold of him before he vanishes or turns into an ant, then I can make him tell me where his treasure is buried. I'll be a rich man, and ride everywhere in my own coach."

So he picked up the sleeping creature and slipped him into the cuff of his greatcoat, feet first, before he could wake.

The little man opened his brown eyes and looked up at Uncle Billy. "Mammy," he cried, "mammy, where are you?"

It wasn't a full-grown spriggan after all but just a spriggan child.

"Where am I?" asked the child. "And who are you?" Then he cried again, "I want my mammy."

Uncle Billy did not know what to do. He said, "I don't know where your mammy is. Why don't you come home with me and wait for her there."

"Can I have milk and blackberries for supper," asked the spriggan child.

"Yes, and bread and honey too," said Billy.

So Billy took the spriggan home, and set him down by the hearth. The child began to play with Billy's own children as if he had known them all his life, and they laughed for joy to see him jumping about. They called him Bobby Griglans, which means "Bobby from the heather."

When Uncle Billy asked him about buried treasure, Bobby said he would happily lead him to it under the next full moon.

For three days they kept Bobby Griglans in the house, and fed him on milk and blackberries. While the house was being cleaned, Bobby would sit on top of the pile of furze and ferns for the fire, and chirrup away like a robin redbreast. When the hearth was swept and the turf fire made up, Bobby would dance for hours on the hearthstone, while Uncle Billy's wife, Mary, knitted away on her stool. The faster Mary's needles clicked, the faster Bobby spun around.

At the end of the three days a group of neighbors came around to help Uncle Billy fetch the cut furze from the hill. Because he did not want them to see Bobby Griglans, he shut him and the children up in the barn and locked the door. "Stay in here and play quietly, like good children," he told them.

While the men fetched the furze, Bobby and the children danced and played in the barn. But as soon as the men had gone in for their dinner, Bobby unbarred the window and called to the children, "Now for a game of hide-and-seek!" They all climbed out of the barn window and began to play among the trusses of furze.

As they were playing, a little man and woman scarcely bigger than Bobby came along. The man was dressed just like Bobby Griglans, except that he was wearing riding boots with silver spurs, while the woman was wearing a green gown all spangled with silver stars, high-heeled shoes with diamond buckles, and a tall blue hat wreathed with heather over her golden curls. She was wringing her hands and crying, "Oh! my dear and tender Skillywidden, wherever can you be? Shall I never see you more?"

Bobby Griglans called out, "Here I am, mammy!"

The woman folded Bobby in her arms; and then she and her husband, and her son, Skillywidden, called by the children Bobby Griglans, vanished as if they had never been.

The children got such a telling off from Uncle Billy for letting Bobby escape. "If we had kept hold of him, he would have shown me where all the spriggans' crocks of gold were buried," Billy said, "and we would all have been rich."

Spriggans are often described as ugly creatures, but not in this case; nor do Skillywidden's parents appear to have taken any revenge on Uncle Billy.

Skillywidden seems to have been perfectly happy to settle in a human home as a kind of part-pet, part-child—at least for a few days. But in fairy time those few days may have seemed no more than a few hours would to us.

There are other kinds of fairies who live right alongside human beings, particularly in farmhouses. They are loyal both to the place and to the family that dwells in it, and if treated well will offer both help and protection. They are also often mischievous, and their attitude toward humans is one of exasperated affection.

In Sweden the household fairy is called a tomte; in Germany, a kobold; and in England, a brownie, hob, or boggart. Often these fairies are hardworking and helpful, but most of them have a mischievous side. They enjoy playing harmless pranks, but sometimes they get out of hand and their antics become a torment to the family that houses them. They are a plague to servants who show them disrespect, pinching the maids black and blue, setting the men at odds with each other, and snatching away food before it can be eaten. Hiding the keys and breaking the crockery are two other tricks of a brownie in a temper.

It does not take much to keep a brownie happy—a bowl of fresh cream and an oatcake at night, and a few kind words are all it takes. But if a brownie's efforts are scorned, he will easily take offence. The brownie of Cranshaws in Berwickshire, Scotland, worked happily for years, harvesting and thrashing the corn, until one year someone remarked that the corn was not well mowed or stacked. The brownie worked all through the night, carrying the cut corn two miles away and throwing it over Raven Crag, muttering,

> It's not well mowed! It's not well mowed!
> It will never be mowed by me again!
> I'll scatter it over the Raven Stone,
> And they'll have some work before it's mowed again!

17

To reward a brownie too generously is equally dangerous. It may be that brownies are somehow tied to a family or a house until they can earn their freedom. When they are rewarded with a suit of clothes, or sometimes just with a name, they depart, never to work again. Sometimes this is because the clothes are regarded as insulting—either they are too poor in quality or a servant's livery.

The most famous English brownie is the Cold Lad of Hilton, who haunted Hilton Castle in Northumberland. Anything that was tidy, the Cold Lad threw about; anything that was messy, he put to rights. This brownie was said to be the ghost of a stable boy who had been killed by his master in a rage. The association between fairies and the dead is very strong, especially in Celtic tradition, where fairies are often said to be spirits of the dead.

Like any ghost, the spirit of the Cold Lad was trapped in this world until it could be laid to rest. He did his work at night, and could be heard singing this sad song:

Woe's me! Woe's me!
The acorn is not yet
Fallen from the tree,
That's to grow to the wood,
That's to make the cradle,
That's to rock the bairn,
That's to grow to the man,
That's to lay me.

At last the servants took pity on him and laid out handsome green clothes to keep him warm. He put them on joyfully, singing,

Here's a cloak, and here's a hood!
The Cold Lad of Hilton will do no more good!

And he was never seen or heard of again.

A Scottish tale tells of a farmer who had a love-hate relationship with a brownie.

THE BAUCHAN

Callum Mor MacIntosh had a small farm in Lochaber in the Scottish Highlands, and he ran it with the help of a bauchan, or house fairy, who did much of the heavy work. But the two of them fell out, no one knows why, and after that nothing went right.

It came to such a pass that one day, when Callum was coming home from market, the bauchan waylaid him outside the house and challenged him to a fight. Soon the two of them were at it hammer and tongs, until at last Callum tripped the bauchan and, while the creature was getting up, ran off into the house.

Once inside he felt in his pocket for his lucky handkerchief, which had been specially blessed by a priest—but it was gone. Callum went back to the scene of the fight to see if he had dropped it. There he saw the bauchan, rubbing the handkerchief against a stone.

"So you're back," said the bauchan. "Lucky for you. For if I had rubbed a hole in this stone before you came back, you would have been a dead man. No doctor or power could have saved you."

"Give me my handkerchief," said Callum.

"If you want it back, you must win it from me in a fair fight," said the bauchan.

"Done!" said Callum.

So they set to again, and at last Callum knocked the bauchan down and took his handkerchief back.

After that they were not even on speaking terms. Callum had to do all the work on his own. Winter was coming and he went into the forest to chop down a birch tree for firewood. But he was so exhausted at the end that he could not fetch the wood home. He simply left it where it was. "I can fetch wood as I need it," he said.

But as the snow fell, Callum's farm became cut off from the outside world. He could not get to the wood, and the few branches he had in the house were soon burned. It seemed as if he must freeze to death. "I wish I had brought home the tree I felled in the forest," he said. Just then there was a great thud at the door. Callum opened up, and there was the birch tree and the bauchan with a great wide grin on his face. And so the two became friends again.

Then there came a time when the landlords wanted to clear the land of little farmers like Callum. Like many of his neighbors, Callum had to leave his home. There was nothing for it but to emigrate to a new country. So Callum said farewell to his farm and to the bauchan, and took ship for America.

When they arrived in New York, the new immigrants had to spend a time in quarantine. As soon as they were cleared to enter America, Callum was the first man off the first boat, he was so eager to start his new life.

As soon as his feet touched the ground, who should he see but the bauchan, in the form of a goat, saying, "Ha! Callum. I was here first!"

Soon Callum found himself a plot in the wilderness, and the bauchan helped him to clear it and turn it into as neat and prosperous a farm as you ever saw.

In Slavic countries, such a house spirit is called a domovoy. The domovoy lives behind the stove and helps the family in all kinds of ways. He can tell the future, and warn the family when misfortune threatens. There is one thing the domovoy can see but no warning can avert, and that is death. When a member of the household is about to die, the domovoy wails and groans, and covers his face with his cap.

Some Irish families also have a fairy who foretells the death of family members by wailing. Such fairies are always female, and are called banshees, from the Gaelic words meaning "fairy woman." The howl of the banshee is not her only way of warning of coming death. In Scotland she may also be encountered at a ford in a stream, trying to wash the bloodstains out of clothing belonging to warriors about to die.

It is said that if a man can get between a banshee and the water before she sees him, she must answer three questions he puts to her—but he too must truthfully answer three questions of hers.

Banshees attached to Scottish families seem to have a wider understanding of their duties than the Irish ones. As well as warning of death in the family, they may perfom all kinds of services.

The banshee of the Macleods of Dunvegan rocked the cradle of the firstborn son; Meg Moulach, the banshee of the Grants, stood beside the head of the family while he was playing chess and showed him the winning moves. As for the banshee of the MacCrimmons, she seems for all the world like the fairy godmother in "Cinderella."

THE BLACK LAD MacCRIMMON

The fairies are excellent musicians, and their favorite instrument of all is the bagpipes; it is the haunting skirl of the pipes that the traveler hears welling from the fairy knoll, tempting him or her to enter and join in the fairies' dance.

Sometimes the fairies have been willing to teach the art of music to some human to whom they have taken a fancy, and the most famous of all these people was the Black Lad MacCrimmon.

Now he was called the Black Lad because he was the youngest of three sons and had to sleep in the chimney corner, so he was always black with ash from the fire. His father and his brothers treated him like a servant.

The father liked nothing better than to play upon the bagpipes, although he was not very good. Then he would hand the pipes to the oldest son, who would take his turn to play, although he was even less skilled than his father. Then it would be the middle son's turn—and he was so

bad that the shrieks of a cat in the night were sweet music
compared to the terrible noise he made. And then the
father would hang the great bagpipes back up and never
let the Black Lad so much as blow one blast into the bag.

One day the father and the two older brothers went to
the fair, and they left the Black Lad at home alone with a
long list of chores to do.

Now when they were gone, the Black Lad picked up
the chanter of the pipes, on which the melody is played,
and tried to blow through it; but all he could do was make
it squeak. He was just about to put it down when the banshee of the castle appeared.

"Would you like to play music, Lad?" she asked.

"Yes," he said.

"And would you prefer success without skill, or skill
without success?" asked the banshee.

"Skill without success," said the Black Lad.

The banshee pulled a hair from her head and told him
to wrap it around the reed of the chanter.

"Now put your fingers on the holes of the chanter," she
said.

23

Then the banshee laid her fingers on top of the Black Lad's and guided him as he played the tune that is called "The Finger Lock," because no one else has ever been able to play it without getting their fingers tangled.

"Now you are the king of pipers," she said.

The banshee left the Black Lad alone with his father's bagpipes. He began to play, and there was not a tune he could think of that he could not play with ease.

When his father and brothers came home from the fair, they heard the music coming from the castle. They were afraid, it was so beautiful. So they waited until the music stopped and then they went in.

That night the father took down the pipes as usual and played a merry reel, nearly at the right speed. The oldest son took over and stumbled clumsily through a tune that should have been lilting and sweet. The middle son also had his turn and produced a collection of wheezes and groans that would make your ears hurt. And then the father, curious about the music they had heard earlier, said, "Black Lad, would you like a turn?"

"Oh, I couldn't," said the Black Lad. "I haven't finished my chores."

"Never mind that," said the father. "You play us a song."

So the Black Lad picked up the bagpipes and played a pibroch, a lament of the Highlands, so lovely and so sad that the eyes of his father and his brothers started running over with tears.

"I shall never touch the pipes again," said his father.

"Nor shall we," said his brothers.

And his father gave the bagpipes to the Black Lad, telling him, "From now on we shall look after the castle and you shall play the music. For your equal has never lived before, nor ever will again."

Banshees stay with the same family generation after generation, and the same is true of other household fairies, such as boggarts. In Germany these household fairies are known as kobolds, and they share some of the characteristics of poltergeists, spirits that make themselves known by knocking and throwing things around.

It was by knocking that the kobold Hinzelmann first made his presence known in the castle of Hudemühlen in the year 1584. Soon afterward he began to talk to the servants, and shortly after that he became confident enough to address the master of the house himself. When conversation got going at the dinner table, Hinzelmann would always join in, though no one could see him.

When asked where he was from, Hinzelmann said he was a forest fairy from Bohemia who had been cast out of his home and sought refuge in the castle. He had quickly made himself indispensable to the household, both upstairs and down. The cook went to bed every evening straight after supper, sure that in the morning all the dishes would be sparkling like mirrors. Hinzelmann worked all night, scouring the pans and polishing the glasses, all for the reward of a drink of buttermilk for his breakfast.

SHOW YOURSELF TO ME

Hinzelmann lived in a little room at the top of the castle, and in it there was a little round table, a bed, and a chair of plaited straw that Hinzelmann made for himself and decorated with all kinds of patterns and crosses. But there was never any sign of anyone having slept in the bed—just a slight depression, as if a cat had been curled up on it.

The master of the house longed to know what Hinzelmann looked like and often begged him, "Show yourself to me." But Hinzelmann always said, "Not yet."

One night, as the master lay in his bed, he was wakened by a rustling noise in his room. Looking across the moonlit chamber, he thought he saw the shadow of a child. "Please," he said, "just this once, show yourself to me."

But Hinzelmann said, "Not yet."

"At least let me take you by the hand."

"No," said Hinzelmann, "for you might catch hold of me and not let me go."

The master promised he would not, and at last he felt the fingers of a child touch his hand; but Hinzelmann drew back so fast, the master only noticed how cold the hand was.

Now the cook was on such good terms with Hinzelmann that she decided to make the same request. "Please," she said, "show yourself to me."

"Not yet," said Hinzelmann.

"What do you mean 'not yet'?" she asked.

"Soon I will let anybody see me who wants to," he said, "but the time is not yet right."

But the cook insisted, so Hinzelmann told her, "If you wish to see me you may. But I warn you, you will regret it. Come to the cellar tomorrow morning before sunrise, and you shall have your desire. But be sure to bring a pail of water in either hand."

"What do I need water for?" asked the cook.

"You will see," said Hinzelmann.

Next morning, just before break of day, the cook crept down to the cellar. It was dark, and she could see nothing. But when the first rays of sun broke through the tiny window, they revealed a naked child about three years old, lying on a tray. Two knives were stuck crosswise in his heart, and his whole body was streaming with blood.

The cook let out a terrible scream and fainted away. Immediately Hinzelmann dashed the pails of cold water over her and revived her.

But though no adult ever saw him again, the children did. When they started playing, often they would find there was one more in the game than when they started: a strange little boy with pale, handsome features and curly yellow hair hanging down his shoulders, dressed in a red silk coat.

After four years Hinzelmann vanished, leaving behind him three presents that he said would bring good luck to the family so long as they kept them carefully: a cross of plaited straw, a straw hat, and a leather glove sewn with pearls. He said he would return in the future, when the family had lost everything, and help them once again.

What type of creature Hinzelmann truly was is hard to say. Perhaps he was originally the ghost of a murdered child, like the Cold Lad of Hilton; the cook's horrible vision would suggest so. When asked if he were a kobold, he denied it, saying, "I am a Christian, like any other man, and I hope to be saved."

Nevertheless, Hinzelmann most probably was a kobold, for he came from the forest, and originally all kobolds were forest sprites. The first kobolds were confined to houses by human beings who cut down their trees and carved them into the figures of little men. Only later did kobolds come to live with human beings of their own accord.

The free kobolds of the forest were probably hobgoblins rather like the English Puck or Robin Goodfellow—mischievous free spirits whose delight was to play tricks on travelers and then leave them with fairy laughter echoing in the wind, "Ho! Ho! Ho!"

Fairy Neighbors

THE FAIRY WORLD is sometimes thought of as somewhere completely different from the human world. The Irish hero Oisín, for
instance, fell in love with a fairy and followed her to the Island of
Youth, where they lived happily until he became homesick for
Ireland. She pleaded with him not to go home, but he insisted. As
soon as his foot touched the ground, all the years that had passed
fell on him at once, and he became an old man. Everyone he had
known was long dead.

Often fairies are said to live in some faraway or impossible-to-find
land, but they are also described as living so close to human beings
that they almost overlap—close enough, for instance, to borrow a
cooking pot when they need one.

In Worcestershire, England, for instance, a fairy once came up to
a plowman and said,

> O, lend a hammer and a nail,
> Which we want to mend our pail.

The plowman was pleased to be of help; and ever afterward, any
woman who broke her peel, or wooden baking shovel, had only to
leave it at the Fairies' Cave at Osebury Rock and the fairies would
mend it for her.

This close relationship between the two communities has encouraged fairies to employ human beings as their servants. They often

employ human women as midwives to attend fairy births, or as nursemaids to the children afterward. The fairy birthrate is not high, and it may be that their children need special care when young—and more attention than the carefree, pleasure-loving fairies would naturally give them. Scottish tradition does, however, preserve several tender fairy lullabies, including one that, imagining a girl searching for her lost cattle up hill and down dale until she is tired out, has a similar rocking motion to the human kind:

> O little Morag,
>   A-climbing bens,
>   Descending glens,
>   A-climbing bens,
> O little Morag,
>   A-climbing bens,
> Tired thou art,
>   And the calves lost.

This was heard by two children who were out feeding their father's cattle, when they put their ears to the side of a fairy hill. It was, they said, the sweetest music that ear ever heard.

One human girl who, all unawares, took service with a fairy family was Cherry, who lived in Zennor in Cornwall.

CHERRY OF ZENNOR

Cherry was sixteen, the youngest of ten children who lived with their parents in a tumbledown cottage on a few acres of scrubland. They had just enough to eat, but no more, and times were always hard.

Cherry was a lively, healthy, happy girl. She could run as fast as a hare, and was always full of fun and mischief. So one day she decided to leave home and seek her fortune. She tied up a few things in a bundle and set off down the road.

Almost as soon as she was out of sight of the cottage, she began to feel homesick but she went on; until she was farther from home than she had ever been before. She

came to a crossroads on the Lady Downs and sat down on a stone by the roadside. She cried to think of her home, which she might never see again.

When she dried her eyes, she looked up to see a gentleman standing there. She didn't know where he had come from, for there hadn't been anybody on the downs a few minutes before.

"Good morning," he said. "Can you tell me the way to Zennor."

Cherry pointed back down the road. "It's that way, sir," she said. "That's where I've come from. I've left home to seek my fortune."

"Have you, indeed?" The gentleman looked her up and down. "You look like an honest girl, and not afraid of hard work. Perhaps I can help you."

He told Cherry that he was a widower with one little boy, and that he was looking for a girl to look after his son for him. "I can see that your clothes are so patched that it is impossible to tell which was the original material," he said, "but they are perfectly clean. And you yourself are as fresh as a daisy. I think you would do perfectly."

"Yes, sir," said Cherry. Her mother had told her, "When a gentleman speaks to you, always say, 'Yes, sir,' even when you can't understand a word he's saying." Now Cherry was glad of her mother's advice.

She followed the gentleman; and as they walked, he talked to her. His stories were so fascinating, she had no idea how far they had gone or how long they had been walking. Whenever he said something she did not understand, Cherry said, "Yes, sir," and he carried right on.

At length they came to a country lane, so shaded with trees that a checker of sunshine gleamed on the road. Sweetbriers and honeysuckles perfumed the air, and the reddest of ripe apples hung from the trees over the lane.

They came to a stream of water as clear as crystal, which ran across the lane. The gentleman put his arm around Cherry's waist and picked her up to carry her across, so she would not get her feet wet.

The lane was getting darker and darker, and narrower and narrower, and they seemed to be going steeply downhill. Cherry was a bit nervous. She took hold of the gentleman's arm and at once she felt better. She thought he was so kind and so interesting, she would follow him to the world's end.

Soon they came to a gate, which led into a beautiful garden. "Here we are, Cherry," said the gentleman. "This is my home."

Cherry could scarcely believe her eyes. She had never seen anything so lovely. There were flowers of every color, and fruits of every kind; and as for the birds, the air was full of their song. It was like an enchanted place.

A little boy came running down the garden, shouting, "Papa, Papa!"

From the size of him, the boy should have been about two or three years old, but he seemed older to Cherry.

His eyes were brilliant and piercing, and they had an odd, crafty expression, as if he knew a secret about you that you did not want him to know. When he caught Cherry's gaze, she had to look away. He could stare anybody down.

Then an old lady appeared—a disagreeable, dry-boned, hatchet-faced old woman, who took the boy by the arm and dragged him into the house, mumbling and scolding the whole while.

"That is Aunt Prudence," said the gentleman. "She has been looking after the boy since his mother died."

Cherry made a face.

"Don't worry," he said. "She will only stay until you have settled in. Then we will send her packing." He gave Cherry a smile to melt her heart.

That night Aunt Prudence showed Cherry to her bedroom at the top of the house, where the boy was also to sleep. She told her, "If you take my advice, you'll shut your eyes and keep them shut, whether you're asleep or not. That way you can't see anything you won't like."

"Yes, ma'am," said Cherry, and "no, ma'am."

"Tomorrow," said Aunt Prudence, "you must rise at break of day and take the boy to the spring in the garden to wash. In a cleft in the rock you will find a crystal box containing an ointment for his eyes; you must put some of it on him, but be careful to wash your hands and not get it in your own eyes. It stings like anything."

After that Cherry was to call the cow, and draw a bowl of milk for the boy's breakfast.

Cherry was very curious about all of this; but when she tried to ask the boy about it, all he said was, "I'll tell Aunt Prudence."

In the morning, Cherry got up at dawn, and took the

boy down to the spring, which rose sparkling and pure from a granite rock covered in soft moss. She found the ointment and rubbed it on the boy's eyes, being careful not to get any in her own. Then she called the cow and drew fresh milk for breakfast.

Afterward she helped the old woman in the kitchen. Aunt Prudence told her she must not go into any other part of the house, and especially must not try to open any locked doors.

The next day was much the same, except this time the gentleman asked Cherry to help him in the garden. They weeded the leeks and onions, and every time they got to the end of a row, the master gave Cherry a kiss to show how pleased he was.

But Aunt Prudence was not pleased. She sat there with one eye on her knitting and one eye on Cherry, muttering and grumbling. Cherry only heard a few phrases. "Chit of a girl" and "no fool like an old fool" were two of them.

The next day Aunt Prudence led Cherry by the hand down a long dark corridor to a locked door.

"Shall we take a look in here?" she asked.

Cherry was frightened, but she was curious too. "Yes," she said.

Aunt Prudence unlocked the door. She made Cherry take off her shoes, and then they stepped inside.

The floor of the room was just like glass. All around the room there were the figures of men, women, and children, turned to stone. Some were perfect, but some were only head and shoulders, or had no arms or legs.

Cherry said, "I don't want to see any more." But Aunt Prudence just laughed. She made Cherry rub a box like a coffin on six legs until she could see her face in it. Every time Cherry flagged, Aunt Prudence called out, "Rub! Rub! Harder! Faster!"

At last Cherry gave such a violent rub that the box rocked over, and from it came such an unearthly wail that Cherry fell down in a faint. She thought all the stone people were coming to life.

The gentleman came running in. He was very angry

with Aunt Prudence, and told her to leave the house and not come back. Then he carried Cherry into the garden and gave her some cordial to revive her. "You've had a horrible dream," he said. "You must have gone to sleep in the sun."

He kept talking to her until Cherry could not remember what had happened. She only knew that she did not want to explore any farther than the kitchen and her little bedroom in the attic.

With Aunt Prudence gone the days passed happily. Cherry thought there was no girl in the world who had a kinder master nor an easier life—except for one thing. Every day she rubbed the ointment on the boy's eyes, and every day those eyes got sharper and brighter, until she almost felt he could see right through her.

So one morning, after she had washed the boy in the spring, and rubbed the ointment on his eyes, and milked the cow for breakfast, she sent the boy off to gather some flowers. While he was gone she rubbed some of the ointment in her own eye.

Oh! She thought her eye would be burned right out of its socket.

She ran to the spring to wash it out. And there, at the bottom of the crystal clear water, she saw a garden just like the one she was in. It was full of hundreds of little people, mostly ladies, playing. There was her master among them, as small as the rest. There were little people everywhere, hiding in flowers sparkling with diamonds, swinging in the trees, and running and leaping over blades of grass.

Her master never showed himself above the water all that day; but in the evening he rode home, just like an ordinary man.

Cherry plucked up her courage and followed him down the long dark corridor. She saw him go to the locked room, and soon she heard wonderful music coming from within.

She put her eye to the keyhole and saw her master with a group of ladies, who were singing and playing music. One was dressed like a queen, and it made Cherry feel

sick at heart to see her master kiss this one.

Next day he asked her to help him gather fruit and, when they had filled the first basket, leaned over to give her a kiss. But Cherry slapped his face and told him, "Kiss the ladies under the water, if you want to kiss someone." And so he found out that she had used the ointment.

"You must leave this place," he said. "I will not have a spy living in my house."

Cherry cried and said she was sorry, and the gentleman said, "I am sorry too."

He called her before dawn the next day, and she took her bundle in one hand and a lantern in the other and followed him. They went for miles and miles, all uphill, through lanes and narrow passages, and at last they came up to the level ground. Then Cherry understood at last that she had been enchanted and that she had been living all this while underground, with the fairy folk.

The gentleman told Cherry, "You may never come among us again. But if you come out to the Lady Downs on moonlit nights, I may come to see you." He gave her one final kiss and disappeared. And the sun rose, and found Cherry seated alone on a rock of granite, without a soul to comfort her.

At last Cherry picked up her bundle and set out to walk the long miles home.

When she reached Zennor, her parents at first thought she was her own ghost; they had long since given her up for dead. When she told them what had happened to her, they thought she must be making it up. But she never changed her story, and at last everyone believed her.

They say Cherry was never the same happy-go-lucky girl again. She had a faraway look in her eye, as if what she was seeing was not quite what other people saw, and on moonlit nights she would wander till dawn on the Lady Downs, looking for her master.

Several similar stories are told in Cornwall. Another story from Zennor calls the girl Jenny, and she acquires fairy sight when her master dries her tears with a fern leaf. Yet another story calls the girl Grace Treva and names the fairy master as Bob o' the Carn.

The great authority on British fairies Katharine Briggs suggests that in these stories the fairy master's first wife was a human woman, and that, therefore, the boy needs the fairy ointment rubbed on his eyes to give him fairy sight. In stories of human women called in to attend fairy births, the midwife is required to anoint the baby's eyes with a special salve. It may be that these are all cases of half-human, half-fairy children, and that purebred fairies do not need it.

In the Welsh story of Eilian, for instance, Eilian is a human girl with beautiful golden hair who goes to a meadow to spin flax by the light of the moon and sees the fairies—the Fair Folk—dancing and singing. She goes with them and is seen no more.

Some time after this a strange gentleman comes knocking at the door of the local midwife and calls her to a cave. Inside is the finest room she has ever seen, and a great lady lying in a luxurious bed. After the birth the husband gives the midwife ointment to anoint the baby's eyes, but warns her not to touch her own eyes with it.

However, her left eye starts to itch, and when she rubs it, she accidentally smears it with ointment. This gives her a strange

double vision. Through the untouched eye she still sees a grand chamber; through the other she sees a bare cave, with the wife lying on a bundle of rushes and ferns by a little fire. And she recognizes the wife as the missing girl with the golden hair, Eilian.

Later, at market, the midwife sees the fairy gentleman again and greets him, asking after Eilian.

"Eilian is well," he answers. "But which eye do you see me with?"

"With this one," she replies, pointing to her left eye.

The fairy takes a bulrush and pokes her in the eye, blinding her, and robbing her of her fairy sight.

There are many similar stories. The ointment, it seems, enables human beings to see through the glamour that fairies cast over them, and which enables fairies to move invisibly through the human world.

Other stories suggest that human children are much more likely to see fairies than are adults, and they are often said to have made playmates of fairy children. In Northumberland, for instance, the story is told of a widow and her only son, who lived in the old days in a little cottage in the border country between England and Scotland.

MY AINSEL

One cold winter night the widow and her young son were sitting by the fire for warmth. Several times she said, "It's time for you to go to bed," but the boy was in a wilful and obstinate mood, and refused to go.

"I'm not sleepy," he said.

"If you don't go to bed the fairies will come and take you," his mother said. But the boy only laughed.

When his mother went to bed, the boy stayed up by the fire, watching the crackling flames cast leaping shadows on the cottage walls.

Soon a beautiful little figure came down the wide chimney and stood on the hearth. It was a girl, about the size of a child's doll.

"Who are you?" asked the astonished boy.

"My Ainsel," the girl replied—My Own Self. She asked in turn, "Who are you?"

"My Ainsel," the boy replied, not to be outsmarted.

They began to play together, like brother and sister, as if they had known each other all their lives.

The fire died down, and the boy took the poker to stir it up. He was careless, and a hot coal fell from the fire and scorched the foot of his fairy playmate. She screamed out in pain, and the scared boy flung down the poker and scampered off to bed.

As he lay cowering beneath the covers, he heard the voice of the fairy's mother asking, "Who has hurt you?"

"It was My Ainsel," said the girl.

"Why then, what's all the fuss about?" asked the mother. "If you did it yourself, there's no one to blame."

The incident in which the hero escapes punishment for inflicting an injury because the injured party thinks his name is "My Self" or "No One" occurs in the ancient Greek tale of Odysseus. This fairy version was widely told in the north of England.

More worrying are the many stories told in Europe of how the fairies coveted human children and stole them in order to breed new strength into their dwindling race. In these stories fairies steal a human child and leave in its place a changeling. At first this looks just like the stolen child but it will not thrive, and soon becomes sickly and wizened.

The mother takes advice from a wise man, who tells her to test the child in some way—sometimes cruelly, by whipping it, or throwing it in water, or pretending she is going to cook it on the stove. This cruel treatment—which was sadly sometimes really tried on ailing children—provokes the child into revealing itself, or provokes the fairy mother into rescuing it.

In the Welsh versions the mother is advised to make soup in an eggshell and say it is to feed the harvesters. The child says, "I have seen the acorn before it was an oak, and the egg before it was a hen; but I have never seen the like of this before." The mother, now certain that her wailing, difficult baby is a changeling (and if it saw the acorn before it was an oak, quite possibly several hundred years old), beats it; and the fairy mother comes to save it, bringing the human child back. The child wakes and says, "Ah, mother, I have been a long time asleep."

In an English version the human mother nurses the changeling baby for twenty-four years, and it never grows, even though it is always hungry and never satisfied.

THE CHANGELING

One day the woman's oldest son came home from the wars, took one look in the cradle, and said, "That is not my brother."

"Yes, it is" said the devoted mother.

"We'll see about that," said the soldier.

He set about brewing ale in an eggshell, making a great performance of it, and the infant in the cradle began to howl with laughter.

"I am old, old, ever so old," it said, "but I never saw a soldier brewing ale in an eggshell before."

While the mother cried and called out for her lost baby, the soldier chased the changeling out of the house with a whip and it vanished out of the door. And there on the threshold, stood the soldier's long-lost brother, twenty-four years old, strong and healthy.

The fairies had kept him, he said, in a fine palace under the rocks and fed him on the best of everything.

"I shall never be so well off again," he said, "but when I heard my mother calling, I had to come home."

Sometimes the fairy changelings seem to have been aged fairies, content to live the easy life, having their needs catered to by a human mother, but sometimes they are said to be fashioned from logs of wood and to be mere imitations of living creatures.

The fairies are also said to have stolen human women and left similar imitations in their stead. Scottish tradition tells how a man named Alexander Harg married a girl coveted by the fairies, and one day on the seashore heard the sounds of carpentering from inside an old wreck. One voice asked, "What are you doing?" and another replied, "Making a wife for Sandy Harg."

All that night Sandy held his young wife close. He refused to answer knocking at the door, or to go outside to see what was wrong when first his cattle seemed to stamp and then his horses screamed as if the stable were on fire. In the morning they ventured out and found, abandoned at their door, a piece of moss oak fashioned to the shape and size of his wife.

This was what the fairies would have left in her place. By their glamour it would have seemed to live for a short while, but soon it would have died, and Sandy's true wife would have been captive forever in fairyland. Sandy took the thing and burned it to ash.

Not all fairy neighbors are malevolent, and there are many stories of humans and fairies living peaceably together. If a human farmer accidentally builds a stable over a fairy dwelling, for instance, he may receive a polite visit from a strange man or woman, asking him to visit their house. Sitting down to a meal, he finds his enjoyment spoiled by the smell from the stable. The fairies ask him to move it. If he does, he finds everything goes well from that moment on; if not, ill luck dogs him.

Even when there is no real cause for friction, natural playfulness can cause a rift between human beings and their fairy neighbors.

In one valley in Switzerland, for instance, it is said that the local dwarfs used to come down from the mountains to help with the harvest every year. Sometimes they worked alongside the men; sometimes they just sat and watched in a spirit of friendly interest, sitting in rows on the branches of a maple tree.

One time some mischief makers crept out in the night and sawed the branch nearly through. When the dwarfs sat on it, the branch broke off, and they all tumbled to the ground. When the people laughed at them, the dwarfs were furious. They stomped off, muttering about the wickedness of humans, and never came down into the valley again.

Fairy Helpers

JUST AS SOME fairies love playing tricks on human beings, so some love to help them. There are many stories of helpful fairies of the house and farm, such as Fenoderee, the most famous of all the fairies found in the Isle of Man.

Fenoderee was larger than the common run of brownies, rather like his English equivalent Lob-Lie-by-the-Fire. He had enormous strength and stamina; and sometimes he seems rather like the Celtic giants, who amused themselves throwing huge stones around. He was in fact one of the ferrishyn, the trooping fairies of the Isle of Man, who was banished from fairyland because he fell in love with a human girl and preferred to dance with her in the merry glen of Rushen than attend the fairy harvest revels. When he was cast out, he was transformed into a wild ugly creature covered with shaggy hair; his very name means "Hairy One."

FENODEREE

No one knows what happened when Fenoderee returned to his human love—no longer a sparkling, elegant fairy, but instead a huge, lumbering, hairy creature. Probably she too rejected him, as his fellow fairies had done when he chose her over them. Certainly he is always described as a solitary being.

The glen of Rushen, however, remained his special place. It was there that he curled up asleep in the daytime, in a secret spot in the heather at the top of the glen.

At night Fenoderee worked at whatever needed doing on the island. He would drive home the sheep—sometimes losing one over the edge of a cliff, it is true, but making up for that by folding in wild goats and hares along with the herd—or cut and gather the hay, especially if he sensed a storm coming.

He did sometimes work in the daytime, especially at harvesttime, when he would set to before daybreak and carry on like a being possessed until the job was done. When he threshed the corn, he was like a whirlwind—his whole body a blur and the air dark with the flying husks. Once a farmer complained that Fenoderee had cut the grass too close to the ground, so the next year Fenoderee refused to cut the hay. He let the farmer do the work himself but followed close behind him, grubbing up the grass by the roots, so fast that the farmer feared Fenoderee would cut off his legs with his scythe. For several years after that nobody dared cut the hay in that meadow, until a soldier hit on the idea of beginning in the center of the field and cutting around in a spiral, keeping his eye open for Fenoderee the whole time.

Once a gentleman wanted to build a great house at Sholt-e-will, at the foot of Snafield Mountain. The stones for the mansion were quarried on the beach, including one large white stone that was so big that all the men in the parish together could not move it. They gave up, saying it could not be done. In the morning they found that Fenoderee had moved all the stones, including the huge white one, up to the building site.

The gentleman was grateful to Fenoderee for this kind help and wanted to do something to show his thanks. So

he had a fine suit of clothes made for him and left them
in the glen of Rushen.

When Fenoderee saw the clothes, he lifted them one
by one, and sang sadly,

> Cap for the head, alas, poor head!
> Coat for the back, alas, poor back!
> Breeches for the legs, alas, poor legs!
> If these are all mine, I can dwell no more
> In the merry glen of Rushen.

Fenoderee gave one lonely wail and vanished, never to
be seen in the Isle of Man again.

The gift of clothes had freed Fenoderee from the spell he was under, but it seems he would rather have stayed as he was, living alone in the glen where once he danced with his true love. It is possible that, having earned his release from servitude to the humans of the island, he rejoined the fairy throng. If so, he was probably a melancholy presence, yearning for the past and cut off from even his memories of happiness. Certainly in the Isle of Man they say that "there has not been a merry world since Fenoderee lost his ground."

Fenoderee was an unusual fairy, because his loyalty was not to a particular family or farm, but to a whole island. But in other ways he behaved very much like the fairy farm guardians who are known throughout Europe. In Scandinavia this creature is called the tomte or the nisse. The tomte is described as the size of a child, with gray clothes, a red pointed cap, and hands with four fingers but no thumbs.

Tomtes are mischievous and like to frighten the maids on the farm by playing harmless tricks on them, such as blowing out their lamps. One maid on a farm in Norway found something in the loft that looked like a big hank of wool. Curious, she put it in her apron to look at later. When she reached inside her apron, out jumped the tomte, laughing his head off.

The tomte does much of the work of the farm, and asks for no reward save food and drink every Thursday and especially on Christmas Eve, when porridge, cakes, and ale must be provided for him. The story is told in Norway of a maid who, for a joke, ate the tomte's Christmas porridge and gave him the empty bowl. He seized her by the waist and danced her around the floor, singing,

> If you eat the tomte's porridge, here,
> Then you must dance with the tomte, dear!

He danced her around and around, singing this song, until she dropped down dead.

Tomtes have been known to steal hay from neighboring farms, and sometimes this leads to fights between them; all that can be seen of the two squabbling tomtes is a whirl of straw in the air. In Sweden a farmer's wife once went into the cowshed very early in the morning and found the tomte there, feeding his favorite cow with hay from a farm many miles away, saying, "Eat it up, my darling; it will make you big and strong." Another cow standing next to it only got a handful of this special hay; and while the first cow grew plump and sleek, the second remained sickly and thin.

Fairies are often said to help humans with their work. The knockers of Cornwall, for instance, would knock to indicate to miners underground where the richest seams of tin were to be found, and also to warn of danger. They were described by one man who saw them as "no bigger than a good sixpenny doll; yet in their faces, dress, and movements, they had the look of hearty old tinners."

One of the German fairy tales of the brothers Grimm tells how a shoemaker became so poor that all he had left in the world was enough leather for a single pair of shoes.

THE ELVES AND THE SHOEMAKER

That evening the poor shoemaker cut out the shoes from his last piece of leather, intending to sew them in the morning. The next day, when he came to his workbench, he found the shoes already made. Every tiny stitch was as perfect as if it had been sewn by a master craftsman. The first customer who came in the shop bought the shoes, and he liked them so much he paid more than usual.

With that money the shoemaker was able to buy enough leather for two pairs of shoes. That evening he cut out the shoes, and the next morning he found two complete pairs, beautifully made. So it went on, day after day, until the shoemaker, once poor, was wealthy and successful.

One Christmas Eve the shoemaker suggested to his wife that they should hide in the shop overnight, to see who it was who had been helping them. They did so, and they saw two little naked men come in and sew the shoes, so deftly and quickly that they could only watch in amazement. The little men never stopped work for a moment.

"Those little men are the source of all our good fortune," said the wife. "We should reward them. They must be cold, poor things; so I shall make them each a suit of clothes and you shall make them each a pair of shoes." Her husband agreed.

The next night they laid the clothes and shoes out on the workbench and hid once again so that they could see what happened. At midnight the two little men came in and found the clothes. They put them on straight away, and began to dance around the room, singing,

> What fine fellows we two are!
> We will cobble shoes no more!

And after that they never came back again, and the shoemaker had to cobble his own shoes.

A Swedish story tells how a lazy girl acquired ten fairy servants to help her with her work.

THE TEN FAIRY SERVANTS

Many years ago there lived in Gotland a family of peasants who had one daughter, Elsa.

Because Elsa was an only child, her mother and father indulged her every wish, and she grew up spoiled and lazy. So when she married, she had no idea how to keep house.

Every time anyone asked her to do any work—if the maid needed help with the baking, or the serving man asked her to make him some food to sustain him through the day, or her husband asked her to weave some cloth—Elsa would just flounce out of the room, shouting, "Why do I have to do everything? You treat me like a servant!"

One morning she threw herself on the floor, sobbing, and cried, "Will no one help and comfort me?"

"Yes," came a voice. "I will."

Elsa looked up and saw a white-haired stranger with a broad-brimmed hat on his head. "Do not be alarmed," he said. "I am Old Man Hoberg. I have known your family for eleven generations. Your first ancestor asked me to be

51

the godfather of his firstborn son. My christening present to him was a bag full of silver, but my riches only made him proud and lazy. Your family long ago wasted the riches, but I see that the pride and laziness remain. Nevertheless I will help you, for at heart you are a good and honest girl."

Elsa looked up at Old Man Hoberg. She wondered if he were going to give her a bag of silver of her own.

"You complain of living a life of drudgery," he said, "but your life is not so hard. You have just never learned to enjoy your work. So I will give you ten willing and obedient servants, who will do everything for you."

With that Old Man Hoberg shook out his cloak, and ten funny little creatures fell out of it and began hopping about the room.

"Give me your hand," said Old Man Hoberg.

Elsa reached out her trembling fingers, and the old man said,

> Hop o' My Thumb,
> Lick the Pot,
> Long Pole,
> Heart in Hand,
> Little Peter Funny Man—
> Go to your places now.

The ten little servants disappeared into Elsa's fingers, giving her hands a queer tingling sensation.

Elsa sat looking at her fingers and wondered what the odd feeling in them was. Then she found herself thinking, "It is already seven o'clock. I shouldn't be sitting here and dreaming; I should be up and doing."

So she started bustling about, cheerfully performing all the tasks that only the day before she had been so reluctant to even attempt.

No one knew what had caused the change in Elsa, but everyone benefited from her hard work. The ten faithful servants in her fingers never let her down, and under her hands the whole household flourished, bringing wealth and happiness to all.

Even the trooping fairies, who are often said to care only for their own pleasure, sometimes take a fancy to a particular human being —often a child or an elderly person—and try to make him or her happy. In Cornwall the tale is told of an old bedridden woman in Penberth Cove, who was a special favorite of the fairies. Her relations called by her cottage once a day with food, but the rest of the time she was left all alone. But no sooner were her relatives out of the door than the fairies appeared, and vied with one another to amuse her.

Little men, dressed in green, each with a blue or red cap trimmed with a feather, and tiny women, with feathered fans, hooped dresses, and lacy petticoats, danced over the rafters and swung among the cobwebs. Sometimes they caught mice and rode them in and out of the holes in the thatch in a merry game of hide-and-seek.

In Devon a similar story is told of the fairies' fondness for a kind old woman.

PIXY GRATITUDE

There was once an old woman who lived near Tavistock in Devon, in the southwest of England. She loved her garden, especially her beautiful bed of tulips.

The pixies loved these flowers too, and by moonlight they would dance and sing among them, and put their babies to sleep in them as if in a cradle. By their magic the pixies made the tulips even lovelier and more lasting than they were before, and gave them a fragrance as gorgeous as a rose.

The old woman would never let a single bloom be plucked from the tulip bed, for she loved to listen to the fairies singing lullabies as they put their children to sleep.

At last the old woman died, and the tulips were dug up and replaced with parsley. The fairies showed what they thought of that by causing the parsley to wither and die.

At night you could hear the fairies singing sad songs as they tended the old woman's grave. No weed ever grew on it, and it was always green and tidy; and each spring it was spangled with beautiful wildflowers.

In this story the fairies' gratitude is essentially for being left alone to enjoy the old lady's flowers, and also a mark of appreciation for a human being who shared their sense of beauty. In other tales fairy help is the reward for particular acts of courage or kindness.

In Denmark, for instance, a fisherman was well rewarded for his kindness to a merman.

THE MERMAN'S SOCK

While out fishing one bitter winter's day, a fisherman turned his boat back to the shore. He was finding it hard to make any headway against the fierce waves, when he saw an old man with a long gray beard coming toward him, riding on a wave. It was a merman.

The merman was shivering, for he had lost one of his socks. "Oh, how cold it is!" he said. The fisherman, taking pity on him, took off one of his own socks and tossed it to the merman, who put it on. Then the two parted, the merman riding his wave out to the wild sea and the fisherman guiding his boat safely back to land.

Some time later the fisherman was out at sea when the merman suddenly popped his head over the side of the boat, and sang:

> Fisherman who gave the sock,
> Turn your ship and sail straight back!

The fisherman heeded the merman's warning, and sailed back to land as fast as he could. He reached harbor just ahead of a terrible storm, so fierce and sudden that many other fishermen were lost at sea that day.

The mer-people are a special kind of fairy folk, who drag drowned sailors down to their coral palaces beneath the waves and keep their souls in wicker cages. For a merman to save a man from drowning is a mark of true gratitude.

Uncle Tony, a fisherman from Cornwall, told how his father once nearly caught a mermaid—or "merrymaid" as he called her—by creeping up on her as she twisted up her long golden hair, sitting on a rock. But just as he reached her, "she looked back and glimpsed him. So in one moment she dived head foremost off the rock, and then tumbled herself topsy-turvy about in the waters, and cast a look at my poor father, and grinned like a seal!"

In some waters the mermaids can also take the form of seals, and these seal-women are known as selkies. Stories are told of marriages between humans and both selkies and mermaids; but these always seem to end in parting and heartbreak, though often the descendants of such a union have special healing powers, and webbed hands and feet that reveal their sea heritage.

Mischievous Fairies

FAIRIES ARE OFTEN referred to as "The Good People," or "The Gentry," or "The People of Peace." These polite names reveal not simply respect but also wariness and fear. Fairies are not to be spoken of lightly, for they are proud, and easily offended. Fairies are powerful and unpredictable creatures, and, therefore, they are also dangerous. Some, such as goblins, are actively malevolent.

Fairies delight in practical jokes, but their idea of teasing can easily turn into torment for the unlucky person who is the butt of their humor. Some fairies are rather like naughty children, always up to some prank or other but not meaning any harm.

The French lutins, for instance, share many of the helpful features of household fairies such as boggarts, but are much less reliable. A lutin will always prefer play to work, and will play with children for hours on end. A particular feature of lutins is their mastery of shape changing. A typical lutin trick is to turn into a horse, tempt a human being into mounting, and then throw the rider into a ditch. Lutins can manifest themselves as spiders, gusts of wind, or flickering flames, though they most frequently appear in the guise of a small boy, or as a little monk dressed in a red habit.

Lutins often braid the mains of horses, plaiting them into what are called in England elf locks; sometimes the fairies are said to use these as stirrups when night riding. Two French girls once spent the night in a stable. When they awoke, they found that their long hair had been tangled into knots by a lutin, and there was nothing to do but to cut it all off.

When a male lutin is feeling amorous, he dresses up as a handsome young man, and struts around the village making eyes at the girls. If you meet him in this mood, you must address him as Bon Garçon—Fine Young Man.

The French verb *lutiner* means "to fool around." Mischief and naughtiness are central to the lutin's character, and the same is true of the English boggart or the Scandinavian nisse. One Danish story tells of the battle of wills between a nisse and a human boy who tried to match him in naughtiness.

THE NISSE AND THE BOY

This nisse was a dutiful and hardworking house fairy, who asked nothing more than a bowl of porridge in the evening for his pains. Everything in the household ran smoothly and calmly. But then a boy with a particularly mischievous nature took service in the house, and everything was turned upside down.

The boy delighted in annoying the nisse. He was constantly playing tricks on him. For instance, one evening he stole the butter that the nisse liked to melt on his porridge. He hid it at the bottom of the bowl, so the poor nisse had to eat all the plain porridge before he found the butter.

That was one joke too far, and the nisse decided to take his revenge. That night the nisse went up to the loft where the boy and the serving man slept, both in the same big bed. He stripped the bedclothes off and looked at them lying there, one tall and gangling and the other small and stocky.

The nisse shook his head. "Short and long don't match," he said. So he grabbed the boy by the ankles and dragged him down the bed until his feet were level with the serving man's.

Then the nisse went to the other end of the bed, shook his head, and said again, "Short and long don't match." He grabbed the boy by the neck and pulled him back up the bed until his head was level with the serving man's.

Whatever the nisse did, he could not make the boy as long as the man; but he kept pulling him up and down the bed and muttering, "Short and long don't match," the whole night through.

By morning the nisse was exhausted with all this pushing and pulling. So the nisse sat on the window ledge, with his legs hanging down into the yard, for a rest.

The dog was in the yard, and as soon as it saw the nisse, it started barking, for farm dogs and nisses are always sworn enemies. The nisse started teasing the dog, dangling his leg just out of the dog's reach and saying, "Look at my little leg! Look at my little leg!"

In the meantime the boy woke up. He looked and felt as if he had been dragged through a hedge backward. When he saw the nisse sitting in the window, he understood immediately that it was the nisse's doing. So he crept silently up behind him; and while the nisse was crowing "Look at my little leg!" the boy pushed him down into the yard, and shouted to the dog, "Look at the whole of him now!"

In this story the boy has the last laugh, but it is rare for a human being to get the better of a fairy in the long run.

Water fairies seem to be particularly tricky to deal with. The fairies of the sea—the mermaids and mermen—are more likely to lure sailors to their death than they are to offer aid and assistance. The fairies who live in lakes, ponds, rivers, and streams are equally frightening.

The neck (or nök or näck) is a kind of Scandinavian water troll. Necks live in rivers, lakes, and fjords; and each one demands a human sacrifice every year. When the time comes for someone to be drowned, the neck can often be heard calling, "The hour is come but not the man." When people hear this cry, they must keep away from water, for if they go too near it they will hear the neck whispering, "Cross over." If they succumb to this voice and jump in, they never surface. Sometimes simply to take a drink of the water from which the voice has come is enough to kill.

Necks can change their shape into many forms. Sometimes they will pretend to be gold or treasure, tricking human beings by appealing to their greed. Often they take the form of a boat or a light-gray horse, and, when the trusting human has climbed on board, drown them. The true shape of a neck is unknown; sometimes they are described as little men with long beards. When a priest at Sund-foss in Gjerrestad plunged his hand into the water and seized hold of a neck, the creature lay cowering before him in the boat like a little black dog. The priest charmed the neck into a cairn of stones, and since then no one has drowned in Sund-foss.

Sometimes a canny peasant manages to slip a halter on a neck while the creature is in horse form. So long as the man never takes the halter off, the neck must work for him and plow his fields. But sooner or later the man always forgets that the animal is no true horse. The moment he slips off the bridle, the neck escapes, never to return.

THE NECK AND THE FIDDLER

The neck is fond of music; sometimes one may be seen on the surface of the water, in the form of a handsome young man, naked to the waist, wearing a red cap, with golden locks dangling over his shoulders and a golden harp in his hand, playing his haunting, melodious music.

Once there was a musician in Sweden who heard that

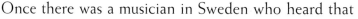

if he left his fiddle on the side of the river, the neck would tune it for him, and then he would never have to tune it again. So he left the instrument on the riverbank; but when he came back, there were two fiddles lying on the grass. One was his own, on which he would play wonderful music; the other was the neck's. If he picked up that one, the fiddle would play music of such power that the very tables and chairs would dance to it.

Luckily the musician had made a secret mark on his own instrument, so he knew which was which. The neck rose from the river and said, "Well chosen, man. Would you like me to teach you the 'Neck's Reel'? It is a tune that has the heart of all music in it."

"What payment would you require?" asked the man, knowing a neck never gave anyone something for nothing.

"Just a drop of your blood," said the neck. So the man took out his penknife and cut his finger, and let the neck suck the blood from the wound. In return the neck taught him many secrets of making music.

61

Some time later the musician was at a party, and the people asked him to play. When he had run through every tune he knew, he decided to play the "Neck's Reel." As soon as he started playing, everyone had to get up and dance. Even the furniture joined in. They danced whether they wanted to or not, and they could not stop.

They had nearly danced themselves to death when a girl came in who had been out feeding the animals.

Luckily she had a four-leaf clover pinned to her clothes, so when she came into the room, she could see the neck himself, sitting behind the fiddler, grinning. She darted forward and cut the strings on the fiddle, for that was the only way to make the music stop. If she had not the fiddler would have gone on playing, and the people would have gone on dancing, until they all dropped dead.

In Scotland, the water horse is known as a kelpie; if you are so foolish as to mount a kelpie, it will plunge into the water and drown you. The kelpie, like the lutin, goes courting in the form of a handsome young man.

One young woman, who was herding cattle on a remote hillside, was joined by a young man who sweet-talked her and fell asleep in the sunshine with his head in her lap. She was falling head over heels in love when she glanced down and saw that instead of feet, the young man had horse's hooves! Gently she moved her legs so that his head was only resting on her skirt and, with a pair of scissors, cut around the material so that she could get up and run away. When the sleeping kelpie awoke and found her gone, his bellows of anguish echoed all around the hills.

THE WATER HORSE

In days gone by a pool on the river Spey was haunted by a water horse, which was the terror of the surrounding country. Sometimes he could be seen feeding with the cattle on the riverbank, and then he seemed to be the most beautiful horse there ever was. His coat was as black and glossy as a raven's wing. On his head was a glittering bridle, and on his back a saddle with stirrups of silver.

If any man was bold enough to approach him, one glance of the horse's fiery eye sent a thrill of terror through him that rooted him to the earth, so that he could not move hand or foot. If, in his fear, the man then forgot to cross himself, the beautiful black horse would draw nearer and nearer to him, and the fierce glance of his eye would change to the mild look of a deer. When he came up to the man, he would fawn on him by rubbing his shining head against the man's chest.

Soon the man's fear would vanish, and he would spring into the saddle; and then, quick as an arrow from the bow, the black horse would plunge into the river. The man would never be seen again, and the horse would not be seen for a year and a day.

The cattle that grazed on the riverbank belonged to a man named Little John of the Yellow Moss. Although he was only a small man, Little John was brave, and he went to a witch to ask how to capture the water horse.

"On May Eve you must kill your speckled ox," she told him. "Dress yourself in its skin and go on all fours to the river meadow. There you must mingle with the cattle. At sunset, the black horse will come out of the water and graze with the cattle. Approach him carefully. If you show the least fear, he will sense it, and your wife will never see you again. Seize hold of his bridle and pull it off. So long as you keep the bridle from him, the horse will be under your control and must do as you say."

So Little John did as the witch advised. His wife dressed him so cleverly in the ox skin that the cows mistook him for the speckled ox that he had killed. When the horse came to graze on the riverbank, Little John, pretending to nibble the grass, got between the horse and the river and then, with a great spring, caught hold of the glittering bridle, pulled it off the horse, and grabbed him by the forelock. "Ha, ha! my lad, I have you now!" he said.

"You have me now, indeed, Little John of the Yellow Moss," said the horse. "If you will show me the same kindness as you show to your other animals, I will serve you faithfully day and night until you give me back my own bridle and saddle by the hand of a maiden; and then I will trouble the country no more."

Little John's wife was terrified when she saw him leading the great black horse to the stable, but Little John told her, "This horse will make our fortune."

There was not a horse in the whole course of the Spey to compare with Little John's black horse. No road was too rough for him to tread, no load too heavy to carry, no fodder too coarse to eat. With the help of the black horse, Little John could empty the Yellow Moss of peat faster than the men of the village could build it into stacks. This went on for years, and Little John and his wife grew rich. Men came from far and near to try to buy the horse, but Little John turned them all away.

One day Little John and his wife went off to the fair, leaving their daughter, Sheena Vane, behind. Sheena used to feed the black horse with her own hand, and loved it dearly.

While her parents were out, Sheena found the bridle and the saddle in the secret place where Little John had hidden them. Thinking that she would go for a ride, she took them to the stable. When the black horse saw them, he neighed with delight. She put the saddle and the bridle on him, and no sooner was Sheena Vane in the saddle than away he went as fast as the wind.

They passed Little John and his wife on the way home from the fair, and the horse cried out, "I have now got my bridle and saddle from the hands of a maiden, and I will trouble no man anymore."

He plunged into an icy lake, with Sheena Vane on his back. At the point where he dove in, the lake never froze over, however thick the ice might be on the surrounding water. On cold winter nights, when the wind blew strong and swept the snow across the hills in blinding clouds, the voice of Sheena Vane could be heard above the roar of the storm. "I am cold, I am cold" was what she wailed— an eerie, piteous cry that sent a cold chill through the hearts of all who heard it.

Fairy Treasure

STORIES ABOUND IN which humans carry home fairy gold that, in the true light of day, is merely a pocketful of leaves or a sackful of straw; and others in which fairies reward humans with stones or coals that turn into coins or gold nuggets. In either case the fairy glamour is at work, making things seem the opposite of what they are.

Many solitary fairies are believed to have a treasure that the brave or cunning may win from them. The korred, for instance, is a kind of Breton dwarf or troll. He has clawed hands like a cat and horned feet like a goat. The korred is a short stumpy creature with shaggy hair and a wrinkled face with dark little deep-set eyes as bright as garnets. Each korred carries a large leather purse full of gold; but if you steal the purse, all you will find inside is a pair of scissors and locks of cut hair.

The Irish leprechaun, the fairy cobbler, does not carry his treasure with him; it is a pot full of gold, buried in the ground. But tradition says that someone who catches a leprechaun can make him divulge the whereabouts of his crock of gold. As the Irish poet William Allingham wrote,

> "Tip-tap, rip-rap.
> Tick-a-tack-too!
> Scarlet leather, sewn together,

This will make a shoe.
Left, right, pull it tight;
   Summer days are warm;
Underground in winter,
   Laughing at the storm!"
Lay your ear close to the hill.
Do you not catch the tiny clamor,
Busy click of an elfin hammer,
Voice of the leprechaun singing shrill
   As he merrily plies his trade?
     He's a span
     And a quarter in height.
Get him in sight, hold him tight,
   And you're a made
     Man!

But it is not quite so easy as that, as we shall see.

THE LEPRECHAUN

Tom Fitzpatrick was the eldest son of a farmer in County Kildare. One fine day Tom was rambling along the sunny side of a hedge when he heard a clacking sound.

"It can't be a stonechat singing," he said. "It's too late in the year." So he craned his head to try to see what was making the noise.

The first thing he saw, lying on the ground, was a brown pitcher. And then he saw the source of the noise. It was a little old man with a cocked hat and a leather apron. He was sitting on a three-legged wooden stool, and he was hammering a new heel onto a shoe.

A leprechaun!

Tom knew that the only way to catch a leprechaun was to sneak up on him, and never take your eyes off him for a moment or he would be gone in a twinkling. So he crept up like a cat hunting a mouse, until he was only a few inches away. Then he said, "God bless your work, neighbor."

The leprechaun looked up. "Thank you, kindly," he said.

"Can I ask you what you have in that pitcher?" asked

68

Tom. He wondered if it was the famous crock of gold.

"Heather ale," said the leprechaun.

"Heather ale?" said Tom. He had never heard of such a thing. "Can I try it?"

"Wouldn't you be better looking after your father's farm than drinking with strangers?" said the leprechaun. "The cows have broken into the field of oats and are knocking down the corn."

Tom nearly turned to look, but then he remembered that a leprechaun will always try to trick you into looking away. So he grabbed hold of the leprechaun and upset the pitcher, so that all the heather ale spilled out, and he never got to taste it.

"If you don't take me to your crock of gold, I'll beat you," Tom said in a theatening voice.

The leprechaun was quite frightened. "Come with me a couple of fields away, and I will show you my crock of gold," he said.

So they went, Tom holding the leprechaun tight by the hand, across hedges and ditches and through a patch of muddy bog, until they came to a field full of thousands of ragwort plants. The leprechaun pointed to one of these and said, "Dig under that plant, and you will find a crock of gold."

Tom, in his hurry, had never thought of bringing a spade. So he took off one of his red garters and tied it around the plant, so that he would know it again when he came back. He asked the leprechaun to promise that he would not touch the garter, and the leprechaun said he would not.

"In that case," said Tom, "you may go, and may good luck follow you wherever you go."

"Good-bye, Tom Fitzpatrick," said the leprechaun, "and may you enjoy what you find."

Tom hurried home, fetched a spade, and ran back to the field as fast as he could. And when he got there, every single ragwort plant had a red garter tied around it, and the leprechaun was nowhere to be seen.

So Tom never found his crock of gold, and the leprechaun had the last laugh after all.

Sometimes the fairies are said to ride ragwort or ragweed stalks like horses. The leprechaun's crock of gold is often said to lie at the end of the rainbow; but although from a distance it seems plain where a rainbow ends, as you get closer, it becomes harder and harder to tell, and in the end it proves impossible. Sometimes it is also said that the leprechaun's purse will always have a coin in it, whenever you reach inside. But the most anyone ever seems to have won from a leprechaun is a single shoe—"the prettiest little shoe you ever saw"—and even that was lost in the end.

The leprechauns learned to brew heather ale in the distant past, when the Danes ruled Ireland, and now they are the only ones who know the recipe. When the Danes were driven from Ireland, a band of Irishmen cornered the last two, a father and son, and promised to spare one of them if he would reveal how the heather ale was made. The father said, "I will tell you," so the Irishmen killed the son. Then the father said, "You may kill me now. My son might have been tempted to tell you the secret of our heather ale, for he was young, with his whole life before him. But I will never tell."

A Danish story tells of a brave farmworker who won a single golden cup from the fairies, part of a great treasure hoard said to be worth "three king's ransoms."

THE ALTAR CUP

Near Aagerup in Denmark, right by the sea, lie the ruins of a great castle, underneath which there is a wonderful treasure that is watched over by a dragon. Once a year, on Christmas Eve, the underground folk hold a great festival there.

One year a brave farm servant rode down to spy on the trolls dancing on the seashore. When he came to a place where he could see what was going on, he stopped his horse and stared openmouthed at the little people as they capered and pranced along the strand.

A troll came up to him and said, "Join the fun!"

He danced with the trolls all night long. It was nearly dawn when he thanked them for their hospitality and remounted his horse to return home.

"Have one last drink before you go!" they said. A maiden handed him a golden cup.

Some instinct warned the man. Pretending to lift the cup to his lips, he dashed its contents over his shoulder. Where it fell on his horse's back, it singed off all the hair.

The man clapped his feet to the horse's sides and rode away across a plowed field with the cup in his hand.

The trolls followed him as fast as they could, but they kept stumbling in the deep furrows. "Ride on the way, not on the clay!" they shouted, but he stayed on the field.

When he neared the village, he had to go onto the road, and then the trolls began to catch up. "If I escape," he vowed, "I will give this cup to the church." And he flung the cup over the church wall, so that it at least would be safe.

He urged his horse on, and at last it entered the village, with the trolls hot on its heels. Just as they were about to catch him, he rode in through the farm gate and slammed it shut in the trolls' faces. Without an invitation the trolls could not follow him, so he was safe. The trolls were so angry, they picked up a huge stone and threw it against the gate with such force that it knocked four planks out of it.

71

The stone can be seen lying in the middle of Aagerup village to this day, though the farm is long gone. The cup was presented to the church as an altar cup, and in return the man was given the best farmhouse in the area.

Sometimes the only treasure to be won from the fairies is one's own freedom. Such was the case with a Scottish girl who was abducted by the fairies while out tending her father's cattle.

THE INEXHAUSTIBLE MEAL CHEST

Once upon a time a young maiden went to drive her father's cattle to the hill. A fairy knoll lay in her path; and as she passed it, she met a band of fairies, with one taller than the rest at the head. This one seized her and, with the help of the others, carried her away into the fairy knoll.

As soon as she was inside, he told her that she could go home, with a servant's wages, as soon as she had baked all the meal in the meal chest into bread.

The chest was only small, so the poor girl thought she would not take long in emptying it. But she was deceived. For although she baked and baked with all her strength, day after day, the chest never emptied. As she took meal out of it, so it filled up again.

At last she gave up and just lay on the floor, crying for her home and family that she would never see again.

In the corner of the fairies' kitchen sat an old woman who had been carried off by the fairies when she was young and had long since given up hope of ever getting out. When she saw the girl crying, she remembered her own misery in days gone by and said, "Every time you bake, you use even the last sprinkling of meal. Do not do that but put the last sprinkling back in the chest. Then it will be emptied in no time."

The girl did as the old woman suggested, and the meal in the chest began at last to dwindle. When it was all gone, she went to the chief of the fairies and asked for her wages and her freedom. "The chest is empty," she said.

"I do not believe you," he replied.

She took him into the kitchen and showed him the empty meal chest. He gave the girl her wages and said, "You may go, with my blessing on your sweet smile."

Then he turned to the old woman in the corner. "But you must stay," he said, "with my curse on your big mouth."

The fairy folk have many secret treasures that they can bestow on humans they take a fancy to. The human characteristics most likely to win approval from the fairies are generosity, hospitality, cleanliness, fairness, and cheerfulness. They also appreciate the ability to keep a secret. In Wales the fairies took a fancy to one young boy for no reason, and every day brought him a few coins as a gift. When his mother found the money, she accused him of stealing and forced him to tell her the truth, and after that the fairies never visited him again.

Those who help a fairy in trouble may expect a reward. For instance, a poor Danish boy named Niels once saved a troll from a werewolf. In return the troll gave Niels a magic hammer that enabled him to become a master smith. Sometimes such fairy rewards stem from pity rather than gratitude. Another Danish boy, afraid to go home because an ox was missing and therefore his master would thrash him, was fed two spoonfuls of porridge by one of the bergfolk, the underground fairies, which gave him such supernatural strength that no one ever dared raise a hand to him again.

In Iceland the poet Gudmund Bergthor wanted something even more valuable from the fairy folk: his health.

THE LAST DWARFS IN ICELAND

When Gudmund Bergthor was born, he was paralyzed all down one side; people said it was because his mother and his nurse quarreled violently over his cradle. Whatever the reason, he was a cripple all his days.

Gudmund was one of those poets whose verse had magic powers, and he often used it to save others from the attacks of ghosts and evil spirits. He very nearly managed to cure himself of his infirmity, as we shall see.

One day Gudmund took his friend Andrès Jónson aside. He told him, "There are now only two dwarfs left in Iceland. One lives in some cliffs to the north, and the other lives in a stone not far from here. This second dwarf possesses a magic ointment that would cure me and break the spell of my infirmity."

Gudmund looked at Andrès very seriously. "I have always found you a faithful friend and one who can keep a secret. Therefore I have decided to ask you to help me. I want you to carry me east to the big stone where the dwarf lives and leave me there. On no account come back to me before night falls."

Andrès agreed, and carried Gudmund to the stone and left him there.

Soon after midday a man arrived in the village, in a state of great excitement, asking for Gudmund.

"I have no idea where he is," said Andrès. "Why do you want him?"

"I have left my daughter at home in terrible torment," replied the man. "A ghost or evil spirit came to her in the night, and she is like a mad thing. I wanted to ask Gudmund's help and advice, knowing he would not refuse to help a man in need. Please, I beg you, if you know where he is, go to him. He is the only one who can help."

Andrès tried to stall the man for as long as he could, but he could see that he was desperate; so eventually Andrès agreed to go and look for Gudmund.

He went to the spot where he had left him and saw that Gudmund's verses had succeeded in charming the dwarf

out of the stone. The dwarf was holding the box of ointment, just out of Gudmund's reach.

When the dwarf saw Andrès appear, he was so startled
that he disappeared back into the stone like a lightning
bolt.

Gudmund turned to his friend and sighed. "I see I am
destined to bear my weakness to the grave," he said, "for
no human power can bring the dwarf out of the stone
again."

Andrès carried Gudmund back to the village, and
Gudmund used his poetic gift to save the man's daughter
from the evil spirit that was attacking her. His gift was
given him to help others, not himself.

Fairy Frolics

MOST FAIRIES, ESPECIALLY the trooping fairies who live in fairy courts and are usually seen in groups, love a party. There are many stories of fairy revels, and what befalls the human beings who interrupt them.

One of the most famous stories is that of the Welshman Iolo ap Hugh.

THE FIDDLER IN THE CAVE

In North Wales there is a famous cave that is said to reach far under the ground. Anyone approaching within five paces of the cave mouth will be drawn in, and lost forever.

This cave was a place of fear and rumor to those living nearby. It was said, for instance, that when old Elias ap Evan stumbled by accident over the threshold of the cave, it turned his hair white.

One Halloween the fiddler Iolo ap Hugh boasted that he would solve the mysteries of the cave. Taking with him bread and cheese and a great quantity of candles, he ventured in.

Iolo never returned. But long afterward, a shepherd was passing the spot when he heard a faint melody dancing up and down the rocks above the cave.

The sound was so jolting, the rhythm so broken, and

the sound so screeching that it was hard to make out the tune.

Then, looking up, the shepherd saw a figure at the cave mouth, capering madly in the moonlight and sawing frantically at his fiddle. It was Iolo ap Hugh, his face pale as marble, his eyes hollow and staring, his head dangling loose and disjointed from his shoulders.

Then Iolo disappeared back into the darkness of the cave, still dancing and fiddling like a man possessed. He seemed to have no will in the matter, but was dragged inside like the smoke up a chimney or the mist at sunrise.

Many years passed and the shepherd was now an old man. One cold December evening he was sitting in church when a strange burst of music from beneath the aisle threw the whole congregation into confusion. The noise passed under the church and died gradually away, until at last it was impossible to distinguish it from the wind that careered and wailed outside the church.

The shepherd recognized the tune immediately as the one that Iolo ap Hugh had been playing at the cave mouth—the tune now known as "Farewell Ned Pugh." If you go to the cave on Halloween and listen carefully, you may hear that tune as distinctly as you may hear the sound of the waves in a seashell. And at Halloween on a leap year a star stands opposite the cave mouth and lights it up; and if you dare you may spy on Iolo ap Hugh, still fiddling and still dancing among the fairy host.

Also in Wales the story is told of two farm boys, Rhys and Llewellyn, who were returning to the farm at twilight when one of them, Rhys, called out, "Stop and listen to the music. Doesn't it make you want to dance?" Llewellyn could hear nothing, but could not dissuade his friend from disappearing into the dark.

Llewellyn went home alone, and in the morning Rhys was still missing. Llewellyn's story was so strange that the farmer even suspected he might have murdered Rhys.

Llewellyn took the farmer and another boy, Davidd, back to the place where the two boys had parted. This time it was Llewellyn

who said, "Hush! I hear the sound of sweet harps." No one else could hear a thing until Llewellyn told his friend Davidd, "Put your foot on mine," and then Davidd too could hear the sound of harps and see the fairies dancing around and around in the fairy ring. There were many of them, all the size of children about three or four years old. And among them one tall, gangly fellow, dancing like an automaton: Rhys.

When Rhys came near him, Llewellyn reached into the circle and pulled him out.

"Why didn't you let me finish my dance?" asked Rhys angrily. "I've only been a few minutes."

Rhys could give no account of his fellow dancers, nor would he believe that he had been dancing all night and all day. After that he was never happy again; he lost all interest in life, took to his bed, and soon after died.

When Davidd, who told this story, went back the next day to see the fairy ring, he found it clearly marked by a red ring around the

edge, where the grass had been trodden down, and by the marks of little heels, about the size of a thumbnail, in the earth. But he never heard the music, nor saw the dancers, again.

Fairy rings—circles in the grass of green fields, often with "fairy ring mushrooms" growing in them—are the dancing places of the fairies; and if you do not wish to be pulled into the dance, they should be avoided. It is said that Welsh sheep are the only sheep that will eat the grass that grows in fairy rings, and that is why Welsh lamb is sweeter than any other lamb in the world.

If Rhys had been left in the ring, he would have carried on dancing until someone chanced to break the spell. As soon as he stepped out of the ring, back into mortal time, he would have crumbled to dust. His sad decline even after being rescued is mirrored in stories from other countries. In Sweden it was said that young Anders danced with the fairy queen herself.

THE ELVES' DANCE

On the island of Sör, when the grass begins to grow in the spring, circles of a deeper green can be seen in the grass, where the elves are said to dance.

One night a servant named Anders was sent out late in the evening to bring a horse in from pasture. In the dark he lost his way, and could not find the meadow where the horse was. Exhausted, he sat down at the foot of an oak tree to rest.

Soon he heard the strains of sweet music. Looking up, he saw many little people dancing in a ring upon the grass. They were tripping so lightly that the grass blades scarcely moved under their feet.

In the middle of the ring stood the elf queen herself, taller and more beautiful than the others, with a golden crown upon her head and her clothes sparkling in the

moonlight with gold and precious stones.

She beckoned to Anders. "Come and dance with me," she said.

Anders rose, bowing, and took her by her beautiful hand.

They danced around and around, whirling, almost flying—Anders had never known such joy.

But then it was all over. The music had stopped. The elves had gone. The beautiful queen vanished in the air, and Anders was left alone at the foot of the oak tree.

From that hour Anders was never the same again. From being a lively and cheerful young man, he became sullen and morose. Within a year he was dead.

This fate is one sad result of mixing with the fairies. For some, such as Anders and Rhys, natural human life seems pointless after the exhilaration of a few hours among the fairies. The story of one Danish girl on the island of Funen illustrates another possibility—one from which Rhys was only saved by the quick-wittedness of his friend Llewellyn.

THE GIRL AT THE TROLLS' BANQUET

A girl went out into the fields one evening; and as she was passing by a small hill, she saw that it was raised upon red pillars, with a party of trolls sitting and feasting beneath it. She was invited in; and it was such a happy party, full of laughter, and singing, and pleasant talk, that she hardly noticed the time going by.

At last, though, she said, "I must go." The trolls begged her to stay just a little while longer, and it was all she could do to tear herself away; but she knew they would be waiting for her at home and wondering where she had got to.

When she got back to the village, she was surprised to find it much changed. Even her own home did not look the same. She lifted the latch and walked in, and a stranger said sharply, "What do you think you're doing?"

She looked around her and saw that everything was different. She said she was looking for her father and mother.

Oh, they died years ago," said the stranger. "Their daughter ran away, and it broke their hearts, poor things."

When she understood that for every hour she had spent with the fairies, a year had passed in real life, the poor girl is said to have lost her mind.

Not every human being who joins in fairy revels is doomed to such misery. For some the experience is wild, exhilarating, joyous. The worst Lord Duffus suffered, for instance, was a little embarrassment, when he was discovered in the wine cellar of a king without any good explanation of how he got there.

HORSE AND HATTOCK

Lord Duffus was walking in his fields in Scotland when he heard a noise like a whirlwind and many voices crying, "Horse and hattock."

Curious, he shouted "Horse and hattock" too.

Immediately he rose into the air and was carried off with the fairies. They came to a dark room, where they passed the night with laughter and good fellowship.

At last Lord Duffus fell asleep.

Next morning he was shaken awake by a stranger, who was gabbling nonsense words at him. He could not understand a word. Then it dawned on him: The man was speaking French.

Lord Duffus was in the cellars of the king of France.

He was brought before the king, bleary-eyed, still clutching the silver cup from which he had been drinking when he fell asleep. He was asked how he came to be there.

"I do not know," Lord Duffus replied. "All I did was cry 'Horse and hattock,' and then I was transported here."

At first the king did not believe him; he thought he might be a common thief.

Lord Duffus told him, "I am no thief." He offered the king the silver cup, saying, "This is yours, I believe. It's certainly not mine."

The king said, "I have never seen it before." He looked closely at the fine, plain cup, and said, "This must be fairy work." He gave it back to Lord Duffus, saying, "Keep this, and hand it down to your descendants, along with the story of your wonderful adventure."

The silver cup, completely plain except for the family arms engraved upon it, was passed down in the family and always called "the fairy cup."

The cry "Horse and hattock" seems to have been the standard cry of Scottish fairies and witches as they took to the air. *Hattock* probably means "hat," or "cap," so the cry means something like, "Hang on to your hat and let's ride!" A seventeenth-century school-boy lost his spinning top when, hearing a similar cry from a whirl-wind, he shouted, "Horse and hattock with my top," and saw it whipped away in a cloud of dust.

There are many variants of the phrase, such as "Hupp, horse and handocks" and "Up hors, up hedik." Sometimes the phrase works as a spell to turn a ragwort stem, or a bundle of grasses, into a steed, which the fairies ride through the air like witches on broomsticks. In the Irish fairy tale of "Guleesh," the boy Guleesh hears the fairies calling, "My horse, bridle, and saddle!" When he imitates them, an old plow beam turns into a fine horse, with a bridle of gold and a saddle of silver. The phrase "Hie over cap!" makes it rise into the air, and Guleesh, like Lord Duffus, goes with the fairies to France.

The fairies carry off the king of France's daughter to be a fairy's bride. By making the sign of the cross over her, Guleesh pits the power of Christianity against the pagan magic of the fairies, and saves her. All the fairy steeds turn back into plow beams, or old

brooms, or broken sticks, or stalks of ragwort or hemlock. The poor girl is struck dumb by a malicious blow from a fairy; but a year later, by once more spying on the fairy throng, Guleesh discovers the secret of a herb that will cure her. When he feeds her the magic potion and restores her power of speech, she accepts his offer of marriage, and they live happily ever after.

The gold bridle and silver saddle of Guleesh's horse are reminiscent of the wonderful horses of the Tuatha de Danann, the grandest of the Irish fairies, who lived beneath the green hills. These horses, says Lady Wilde (mother of the playwright Oscar), were "fleet as the wind, with the arched neck and the broad chest and the quivering nostril, and the large eye that showed they were made of fire and flame, and not of dull, heavy earth."

Fairies are often described as riding horses, both on the ground and in the air, and rarely as flying with wings. The gossamer wings of fairies in conventional illustrations are an indication that these are spirits of air not earth. They may also hark back to the old idea of fairies as fallen angels.

What the fairies dislike above all is to be spied on, as the story of the little people of Eilenburg, in Germany, shows.

THE WEDDING OF THE LITTLE PEOPLE

The fairies of Eilenburg wanted to celebrate a wedding. So they slipped through the keyhole and the window slits into the great castle, and began to dance, jumping up and down on the floor "like peas on a barn floor."

The noise woke the old count, who rose from his four-poster bed and went sleepily downstairs to see what was happening. He was amazed to see all the little people, dancing away.

One of them, who was dressed as a herald, approached the count and asked him politely to join in the party. "We only make one request," he said, "and that is that you alone should witness our festivities, and none of your people should spy on us."

The count readily agreed. A tiny woman took his hand and led him in the dance. The room was lit by little torches, and the people were dancing to the music of a fairy orchestra that sounded to the count like the song of crickets. The count could hardly keep up with his partner, who whirled and twirled so lightly around the room.

Suddenly, in the middle of a spritely dance, everything fell still. The music stopped; the dancers froze in their tracks. Only the count lumbered on, trying to keep up with his nimble partner, and breathing heavily.

The fairy bride and bridegroom were pointing up to a hole in the ceiling of the great hall. Everyone looked up. There, looking down at them, was the old countess, staring at them in a fever of curiosity.

The herald bowed to the count and thanked him for his hospitality. "But since our wedding has been disturbed by another eye gazing on it, the race of Eilenburgs will never again number seven people in it.

Then the fairies slipped away through slits and crannies and mouse holes, leaving the count alone in the dark, silent hall.

The curse has lasted ever since; and whenever there are six living knights of Eilenburg, one of them dies before the seventh is born.

In England fairy fairs and markets have often been reported. Though not usually so sinister as the one in Christina Rossetti's great poem "Goblin Market," they do not always welcome human onlookers.

Blackdown Hill, near Pitminster in Somerset, for instance, was the regular market for the fairies around about Taunton. These fairies resemble men and woman much like ourselves, only small in stature, dressed in old-fashioned outfits of red, blue, or green, and wearing high-crowned hats.

THE FAIRY FAIR

One man, who lived at Comb St. Nicholas nearby, was riding home one day when he saw a great company of country folk on Blackdown Hill, mingling with one another. There were all sorts of stalls, and peddlers, and booths for eating and drinking.

At first the man thought it must be a human fair, but then he remembered the stories about the fairies. He decided to ride in among them and see what they were doing. But although he could see the fair plainly from a distance, when he came closer, it became indistinct; and when he was riding through the place where he had seen it, he could see nothing. But he felt that he was being jostled and pushed as if by a great invisible crowd.

Only when he rode out the other side and looked back could he see the fair again.

The man rode home, in some pain; and when he got down from his horse, he found he was lame all down one side, which lasted the rest of his life.

This man's curiosity was rewarded by infirmity—the partial paralysis that was known as "fairy stroke" or "elf stroke." The word *stroke* is still used today for this ailment, caused by the rupture of a blood vessel in the brain. It used to be thought that it was caused by the person having been struck by a fairy or shot with a fairy arrow.

As a contrast to this, the most recent account of a fairy fair that I know caused no ill effects to the two humans who attended it, merely leaving them with a memory and a mystery.

These two, a man and a woman, both relatives of mine, were driving through the Berkshire countryside on a summer's evening some time in the 1960s, when, driving around a corner on a country lane, they came upon a country fair.

They stopped the car and went to have a look. It was a wonderfully old-fashioned fair, with all the flavor of a fair from before the First World War. They thought it must be a historical reconstruction set up for some local celebration.

They were surprised that there were no other people there, but the fair seemed to be open. They were welcomed with merriment by the stallholders, who encouraged them to have a go at every game and taste every sweetmeat.

At last, they left the fair and drove home.

The next day, curious to have another look at the fair, they drove back to the same spot. There was no fair, and no sign on the grass that there had even been one—no mud, no mess, no rubbish. Not a mark.

They drove on to the nearby village and inquired. "No," they were told. "There's not been any fair around here."

They described the field.

"Oh," they were told. "There used to be fairs there, in the old days. But not for years now."

Fairylands

THE FAIRIES, AS we have seen, are fond of human children, often enticing them to fairyland and sometimes keeping them there. It even seems to be possible for a human being, especially a child, to actually become a fairy.

In a book describing a journey through Wales in 1188, Gerald of Wales records one of the most poignant stories of a child lured to fairyland by the fairies (the Welsh Tylwyth Teg), and later spurned by them. The child's name was Elidyr; he grew up to be a priest and was well known to Gerald's uncle David Fitzgerald, the bishop of St. David's. Whenever the bishop questioned him about his story, Elidyr, even as an old man, would burst into inconsolable tears.

ELIDYR AND THE GOLDEN BALL

When Elidyr was about twelve years old and learning to read, he once ran away from his lessons to play by the river. Fearing his teacher's anger, he stayed away, hidden in a hollow by the riverbank, for two days.

As he lay there hungry and miserable, two little men appeared to him. "If you will come with us," they said, "we will take you to a land where there is no work, only play."

Elidyr was very willing to go with them. He followed them through a dark underground tunnel, which emerged into a beautiful country of rivers, meadows, and woodland. The only thing that spoiled its beauty was that the weather was always overcast, never sunny, and the nights were pitch black, for there was no moon or stars.

The two little men took Elidyr to the court and introduced him to the fairy king. The king welcomed Elidyr and told him to play with his son, who was still a child.

All the men of the court were very small, but handsome. Their skin was fair, and they wore their hair long. They rode horses about the size of grayhounds, but they did not go hunting, for they never ate meat or fish. They lived on milk dishes flavored with saffron.

These little people looked after Elidyr as if he were their own. They had no organized religion, but instead worshiped the truth. They never dreamed of telling an untruth or breaking their word, and when they visited our world were always shocked at the way greed and ambition led humans to cheat and lie.

Nevertheless they let Elidyr come back through the tunnel as often as he wished to visit his mother. He told her all about the wonderful new world where he was living and the people who lived there. When he mentioned how many things there were made of gold, she refused to believe him. "But it's true," he said.

"In that case," Elidyr's mother replied, "next time you come to see me, you must bring me something gold as a present."

Poor Elidyr did not know what to do. He did not want to steal from the little people; but he did not want his mother to think him a liar.

So the next day, when he was playing catch with the king's son, idly tossing a golden ball to and fro, Elidyr seized the ball and ran off with it, up through the tunnel, all the way to his home, with two fairies in hot pursuit.

When he got to the door, Elidyr tripped and fell headlong over the threshold, dropping the golden ball. The fairies snatched up the ball and carried it away.

As they left, they spat at Elidyr and shouted insults at him. His face glowed red with shame, for he realized he had betrayed their trust.

He ran after them, trying to apologize, but he could not catch them. Nor could he ever again find the entrance to the tunnel that led to fairyland, though he searched the banks of the river every day for a year.

As an old man, Elidyr could still remember many words of the little people's language, which he had picked up quickly, as children do. For instance, the fairy word for "water" was *ydor*. When the fairies wanted water, they said *ydor ydorum*; when they wanted salt, they said *halgein ydorum*.

There is a kind of companion story to this in the medieval chronicles of Ralph of Coggeshall and William of Newbridge, concerning two fairy children who stumbled by mistake into our world, sometime in the reign of King Stephen in the twelfth century.

THE GREEN CHILDREN

In Suffolk, at St. Mary's of the Wolf-pits, two children were found huddled together at the mouth of a pit—a brother and sister—weeping bitterly. They were shaped just like humans, but their skin was tinged with green, and no one could understand a thing they said.

They were brought to the house of a knight, Sir Richard de Calne. Bread and meat were set before them, but they would not touch it, though they looked to be starving. They refused all food until at last they were offered some beans that had just been harvested, which they ate with delight. Beans were the only thing they would eat.

The boy was always listless and sad, and never thrived;

it was not long before he died. But the girl was stronger, and lived. Slowly she got used to different kinds of food and began to lose her green color. She was baptized, and lived for many years as a servant of Sir Richard.

When asked where she had come from, the girl said that in her homeland all the people were green in color, and that the country had no sun but was always in twilight. She and her brother had been tending their flocks, she said, when they heard a wonderful ringing of bells. Following the sweet sound, they wandered upward through a cavern. When they emerged into the air, they were struck senseless by the bright light of the sun and lay in a faint for a long time. When they were discovered by the people, they were terrified and tried to flee; but they could not find the entrance to the cavern.

Ralph of Coggeshall tells us that he often heard about this girl from Sir Richard de Calne; apparently she was an excellent servant. It is said that she eventually married a man at Lenna, but whether she left any descendants, the legend does not say.

Ralph seems to have shared the story with William of Newbridge, who tells us that at first he did not believe it, but having made his own inquiries, he was satisfied of its truth. The girl, he says, called her own country St. Martin's Land, and claimed that its inhabitants were Christians.

These fairy children seem to have simply got lost and been unable to find their way home. Other fairies have been trapped in our world by enchantment, such as Hildur, the Icelandic fairy queen.

HILDUR, THE FAIRY QUEEN

Once there lived a farmer in the mountains who was unmarried but was looked after by a housekeeper named Hildur. She looked after everything on the farm, and everyone liked and admired her; but no one, not even the farmer, knew a thing about her.

The farm flourished and everything went well, except

that the farmer had terrible trouble hiring a shepherd. This was not because the work was especially hard, or the pay and conditions especially poor, but because no shepherd the farmer employed ever lived more than a year

On Christmas Eve, everyone went to the midnight service in the church except for Hildur, who stayed behind to take care of the house, and the shepherd, who did not return from tending his flocks until too late to set out for the church, which was some way away from the farm. Without fail the shepherd was found dead in his bed on Christmas morning, without a mark on him.

At last the farmer declared he would hire no more shepherds. "The sheep must fend for themselves," he said.

Shortly afterward a shepherd came to the farm, asking for work. He looked strong and hardy, but the farmer refused to take him on. "I am not so desperate as that," he said.

"Have you already hired a shepherd?" asked the man.

"No," said the farmer. "But you must have heard what a terrible fate befalls every shepherd I hire."

"That does not worry me," said the man, "so it should not worry you."

At last the farmer was persuaded, and took the man on.

Everyone liked the new shepherd, who was an honest and open fellow, and on Christmas Eve they went to church with fear in their hearts.

The shepherd finished his work on that night, ate his supper, and went to bed. But remembering what had happened to the other shepherds, he decided to stay awake.

He heard the farmer and the rest of the household come home from church and go to bed; still nothing out of the ordinary had happened. Whenever he closed his eyes and felt himself drifting off to sleep, he forced them open again.

At last he heard the sound of footsteps creeping up to his bed. He glanced that way and saw the figure of Hildur, the housekeeper. The shepherd pretended to be asleep.

He felt Hildur place something in his mouth, like the bit of a horse's bridle. And that was what it was: a magic bridle. She dragged him out of bed with it, mounted on his back, and rode him through the air till they arrived at the lip of a great hole in the earth.

There Hildur dismounted and tied the bridle to a stone. Then she leaped into the hole.

The shepherd did not want to stay tied up all night, and he was desperate to find out what was going on. After a struggle he got the bit out of his mouth, and freed himself. Then he followed Hildur.

He went down and down through the dark, occasionally catching a glimpse of Hildur below him, until he came to a land of beautiful green meadows. He kept tailing Hildur and soon came to a magnificent palace. The doors opened to let in Hildur, and he slipped in unnoticed behind her.

Hildur was warmly greeted by a man dressed like a king and three children who ran up to her, crying, "Mother!" Everyone else in the palace bowed to her as to a queen. They dressed her in royal robes and loaded her with costly rings and bracelets.

The shepherd followed the crowd into a great hall

hung with rich tapestries, with tables laid with gold and silver, and wonderful dishes and wines that made his mouth water.

Hildur sat down on a throne beside the king, and the feast commenced. Everyone there seemed very merry—singing, dancing, and telling jokes. Only the king and Hildur seemed downcast. They sat on their thrones, talking in low voices and never once smiling.

The three children came into the hall and clung around their mother's neck. The youngest was restless, so Hildur set him on the floor and gave him her golden ring to play with. The child rolled the ring along the floor and, as it passed him, the shepherd snatched it up and hid it in his pocket.

At the end of the evening Hildur got up to go, and now everyone seemed sad, except for one ugly old woman who had sat in the corner with a scowl on her face all night.

Now the king approached this old woman and said, "Mother, please, lift your curse. Let my queen stay and live with us."

"Never," said the old woman, through clenched teeth. "Never."

The shepherd hurried back the way he had come and was standing patiently, in the magic bridle, when Hildur returned to ride him home through the air.

She left him back in his bed, saying, "I am sorry to have taken your life; it was not by my own will."

In the morning when the anxious farmer ventured into the shepherd's room, he discovered to his joy that the man was not dead, but perfectly well.

Everyone gathered around anxious to know what had happened in the night.

"Did you see or hear anything in the night?" asked the farmer.

"No," said the shepherd. "But I had a strange dream." He told the household everything that had happened, as if it were a dream. People started looking askance at Hildur, and nudging one another, and moving away from her.

At last she spoke. "I say you are a liar, unless you have some proof of what you say."

The shepherd reached into his pocket and drew forth the ring. "Here is my proof," he said. "Is this not your ring, Queen Hildur?"

"It is!" said Hildur. "And with it you have broken my mother-in-law's evil spell, which has forced me to labor here in the upper world, and only visit my husband and children once a year, on Christmas Eve. On that night I placed a magic bridle on the herdsman and rode him to elfland, and back again. Every year up to now, the strain has been too much for the poor man's heart and each one has died. But this man has had the courage to follow me to elfland and gather proof that I am its queen. And that is all I need to break my mother-in-law's vengeful spell, which she laid on me in anger for daring to marry her son, since I only come from a humble family. The shepherd is the first human ever to dare to enter elfland, and I shall reward him for his courage. But now it is time for me to go." And with that Hildur disappeared, never to be seen in the upper world again.

As for the shepherd, he left the employ of the farmer and started his own farm, which prospered so well that he soon became one of the richest men in the country. Whenever anyone asked him the secret of his success, he said, "It is all thanks to Hildur, the queen of the elves."

Other fairy queens have chosen human men to be their consorts. In Scotland, for instance, the legend of Thomas the Rhymer, a poet who lived in the thirteenth century, tells how Thomas was courted by the queen of the fairies and taken by her on her milk white steed to fairyland, to serve her for seven years.

On the way the fairy queen showed Thomas three roads: a narrow road, thick with thorns and briars, which was the road to heaven; a broad road, level and straight, which was the road to hell; and a winding path among the ferns, which was the road to fairyland.

She warned him not to speak while he was in fairyland or he

could never leave. After seven years Thomas returned to the human world, blessed with the gift of prophecy and a tongue that could not lie.

Thomas lived for many more years in his home at Ercildoune, and foretold many things that later came to pass.

When he was an old man, a hind and a doe came out of the forest to his castle. They led him back under the enchanted trees, and he was never seen again, save by those who visited fairyland and saw True Thomas there.

It is said that Thomas became the trusted councilor of the fairies, and their intermediary with the human world; in Strathspey in the sixteenth century, for instance, he engaged two traveling fiddlers to play at a fairy banquet. When they left the fairy castle, they found the whole scene changed; everyone was wearing outlandish clothes, and they themselves were dressed in ancient rags. Eventually one old man told them, "I know who you are. You are the two fiddlers who lodged with my great-grandfather a hundred years ago and were decoyed into the fairy castle by Thomas the Rhymer." The two men went to the church to give thanks for their escape from fairyland, but at the first words of holy scripture they crumbled into dust.

It is interesting that the gift of the fairy queen in turn for Thomas's seven years' service was a tongue that could not lie, rather like the fairies in the Welsh tale of Elidyr. One legend says that Thomas was freed after seven years because every seven years the fairies had to pay a tithe to hell, and the fairy queen feared that it would be Thomas.

The Scottish ballad of "Tam Lin" tells how a human girl, Janet, takes Tam Lin to be her lover. He tells her that he too was once a human, until he was caught by the queen of the fairies and taken by her to live in a fairy hill. He says,

> And pleasant is the fairy land,
> But, an eerie tale to tell,
> At the end of seven years
> We pay a tithe to hell.
> I am so fair and full of flesh,
> I'm feared it be myself.

Tonight, Tam tells Janet, is Halloween, when "the fairy folk will ride." If she wishes to save him she must wait at Miles Cross to watch them pass and pull him from his horse.

The fairy queen turns Tam Lin into a snake, a bear, a lion, a red-hot iron bar, but Janet holds him tight. At last he turns into a burning coal. As he has instructed her, Janet throws him into the waters of the well, and he emerges, a naked man. She has won him, and all the fairy queen can do is curse Janet for stealing away "the bonniest knight in all my company."

A Cornish tale of a man who lost his sweetheart to the fairies has a sadder ending. It is one of several similar tales; in another, a farmer named Richard Virgo visits an underground fairyland, in which the fairies are playing with a silver ball.

THE FAIRY DWELLING ON SELENA MOOR

Mr. William Noy was a farmer, an honest, good-natured man, well liked by his workers, but not someone you would accuse of poetry or dreaming. He had one secret sadness. His sweetheart, Grace Hutchens, had died three or four years before. He knew he would never find another love like her.

One late summer evening he was taking a shortcut home across Selena Moor—a wild, boggy place—when he saw lights in the distance, and heard the sound of music. It seemed to be coming from a farmhouse, though he could not remember a farm thereabouts.

Mr. Noy went to investigate. He walked through a beautiful orchard toward the house, outside of which he saw hundreds of people either dancing or sitting, feasting at tables. They were all dressed in fine clothes, but they were quite small, and their tables and cups were small too.

Near them stood a girl in white, taller than the rest, who was playing a tambourine for the dancers. She seemed familiar to him in the flickering candlelight.

When she saw Mr. Noy, she gave her tambourine to a man and came toward him. "Come with me into the orchard," she said.

There, in the quiet starlight, he saw that she was his lost sweetheart, Grace.

Mr. Noy was so amazed he thought his heart might stop.

"Thank the stars, dear William," she said, "that I am here to warn you. Do not for your life eat or drink anything in this place, or you will be changed into the small people's state, as I have been. You must have thought I had died, for the small people will have left a changeling in my place; but I am not dead. I am still your true sweetheart."

Mr. Noy was so overwhelmed with joy, he would have kissed her, but she said, "Don't touch me. And do not eat, drink, or so much as pluck a flower in this place, if you wish to see your home again."

"But, Grace," he said, "whatever happened to you?"

"I was taking a shortcut across the moor to see you," she replied, "when I lost my way. I must have been pixy led. Eventually I found this place. I was worn out with hunger and thirst, and I plucked a beautiful golden plum from one of the trees and bit into it. But it was not sweet, it was bitter; and as soon as I tasted it, I fell down in a faint.

"When I awoke, I was surrounded by a crowd of the little people, all laughing at me and telling me I must be their servant now, for I had tasted fairy fruit. They needed a strong girl, they said, to brew and bake, and to look after the mortal babies they stole, for they have few babies of their own these days."

Sure enough, Mr. Noy could hear fairy voices calling, "Grace, where are you? Grace, come here, and be quick about it!"

"What kind of creatures are they that you serve?" asked Mr. Noy.

"They worship the stars," said Grace. "And they are old, thousands of years old. They are tired of life, I think. They have not seen or felt anything new for so long." She pointed to the beautiful apples hanging from the trees. "All their pleasure is in their memories, and those are nearly as dried up as these fruits."

"What do you mean?" said Mr. Noy. "They look delicious." He reached out to pluck one of the ruddy, juicy apples.

Grace snatched it from his grasp. "If you bit into that," she said, "you would find it sour and old, and you would be trapped here forever, just like me."

"But is there no way I can free you?"

"No," she said. "But I am happy enough now. For whenever I have some free time, I can turn myself at will into a little bird, and fly about near you."

She answered the call of the fairies, who were yelling for more food and drink, and Mr. Noy followed her. He had a plan. He knew that if you want to confuse the fairies and break their spells, you must turn your clothing inside out. So he took off his hedging gloves, turned them inside out, and threw them among the fairies.

Instantly they all vanished, and Grace with them. Mr. Noy found himself standing alone in a ruined barn by an ancient orchard of withered trees. Then something seemed to hit him on the head, and he fell to the ground.

There he was found by the people who had gone to search for him, for he had been missing for three whole days.

He was never the same again, and seemed to lose all interest in life, except when a little bird flew by, when he would ask, in an agitated voice, "Is that you, Grace? Is that you?"

Sometimes humans have been content to throw in their lot with the fairy folk. One poor girl in Germany, for instance, was passing a hill one day when she heard the sound of a dwarf hammering and singing inside. She said aloud, "I wish I could live snug underground like that and sing all day, instead of working so hard and never having a moment to myself." A voice came out of the hill, and said, "Would you like to live with me?" "Yes," the girl replied, "I should." Instantly the dwarf came out of the hill, offered her his hand, and told her, "What's mine is yours." So she went to live with him under the hill, and lived very comfortably with her dwarf husband.

English legend also tells of a poor girl who wanted to marry one of the fairy folk. Her name was Anne Jefferies, and she was born in St. Teath in Cornwall in 1626, the daughter of a laborer.

ANNE JEFFERIES AND THE FAIRIES

When Anne was nineteen, she took service in the family of a gentleman. She was a bright, brave girl, who was never frightened of anything or anyone. The other servants used to talk in low voices of the fairies, and say, "I'd be scared to meet a fairy."

But Anne just said, "I would like to have a fairy for my sweetheart."

She walked out in the evenings, turning over the fern leaves and looking into the bells of the foxglove flowers, chanting,

> Fairy fair and fairy bright,
> Come and be my chosen sprite.

She never allowed a moonlit night to pass without going down into the valley and walking along the stream, singing,

> Moon shines bright, water runs clear,
> I am here, but where's my fairy dear?

Just as the humans were nervous of the fairies, so the fairies were shy of the humans, and no fairy ever answered these calls. But they listened to them, and followed Anne about, jumping from frond to frond of the ferns, just out of her sight.

One day Anne, having finished her morning's work, was sitting in the arbor in the garden when she thought she heard someone moving in the branches overhead, as though trying to peer in at her. She thought it must be the young man who was paying court to her, so decided to pretend not to notice. She just went on with her knitting, and the only sound was the click, clack of her needles one upon the other.

Then she heard a low suppressed laugh, and further rustling among the branches.

Click, clack went the needles. Click, clack, click. Anne was vexed that the young man would not show himself, so she muttered pettishly, "You may stay there till the

moss grows on the gate before I'll come to you."

There was immediately a ringing laugh. It was not a man's laugh, but a bright, musical laugh. Though it was a sunny day, Anne felt herself shiver.

She shut her eyes briefly, and when she opened them, she saw six little men, all dressed in green, standing at the entrance to the arbor. They were handsome little figures, with smiling faces and bright, piercing eyes.

One of them, who was wearing a red feather in his cap, stepped in front of the others and bowed.

Anne reached down her hand as if to shake hands, and he stepped bold as brass into her palm. She lifted him into her lap, and he climbed up and kissed her neck, her lips, and her eyes. Then the others followed suit.

One of them ran his fingers over her eyes, and she felt as if they had been pricked with a pin. She was blind.

She felt herself being whirled through the air at a great rate. Then one of the little men said something that sounded like, "Tear away!" and she could see again.

Anne was in the most beautiful place. There were palaces of gold and silver set among orchards laden with fruit, gardens bursting with flowers, and lakes full of gold and silver fish. Even the air was alive with birds of every color, each singing a lovelier song than the last.

Hundreds of ladies and gentlemen were walking about or idling in some luxuriant bower, enjoying the exquisite scent of the flowers. Hundreds more were dancing and playing games.

The six men who had brought her to this place were standing by her, but they were no longer tiny; they were the same size as she was. They were all dressed in the finest clothes, and so was Anne. She could hardly believe she was herself, she looked so grand. The six men followed her everywhere, and seemed to be arguing about who should speak to her first.

The man who had first climbed into her hand took Anne aside into a secluded part of the gardens and kissed her. She never wanted it to end.

But suddenly the other five came upon them, with drawn swords, and stabbed him to the ground in a jealous fury. He lay wounded at her feet, and she screamed.

The fairy who had blinded her before ran his fingers over her eyes again, and all went dark.

Then Anne felt herself whirling about and about, and heard a strange buzzing noise as if a thousand flies were circling around her head.

When she opened her eyes, she was back in the arbor, with many anxious faces about her. Thinking she had fainted, they carried her into the house to recover.

"Where have the fairies gone?" she asked.

"There now, dear, you rest quiet," they answered.

"They are just gone out of the window," she cried. "Did you not see them?"

"Poor girl," they said. "She has had a fit, and her wits are wandering."

After her fairy adventure Anne became famous as a prophet and a healer. People went to her from all over Cornwall, and even as far away as London, asking her to cure them of their illnesses. She did so with medicines she was given by the fairies, who were always with her, though invisible. She never accepted any money for this. It was said that Anne could also make herself invisible at will, and that then she used to go and dance with the fairies.

The fairies fed her on their own food, and she did not need human sustenance; that year she gave up eating from harvesttime to Christmas Day, with no ill effects. The next year she was arrested on suspicion of witchcraft by the famous justice of the peace John Tregeagle, whose wicked spirit is fated never to rest and still haunts the wild coast of Cornwall. He locked her up without food or drink, but the fairies still fed her.

Eventually Anne was freed, took service again near Padstow, and married a local man, William Warren. When she was seventy years old, she was interviewed by a man named Humphrey Martin and at first denied all knowledge of the fairies or of ever having cured anybody.

When asked why, she replied, "If I told you about it, you would put it in a book or a ballad, and I would not have my name spread about the country in books or ballads for five hundred pounds."

But she eventually relented and told Humphrey Martin her story, and even gave him some fairy bread to taste. "I think it was the most delicious bread that ever I did eat, either before or since," he wrote.

In the end this taste of delicious bread tells us all we really know about the fairies—that for all their tricks and deceits, they represent a kind of perfection for which we yearn.

In 1877 the great folklorist Alexander Carmichael asked a man named Angus McLeod, of the island of Harris, whether he had ever seen a fairy. Angus had not, but his mother had, when she was a girl out milking the cows in the sheiling, the pasture where they were grazing for the summer. Her account, remembered with such beautiful poetry by her son, gives us one last glimpse of the fairy folk, dancing in the Celtic twilight and singing a song as pure and enchanting as that of the song thrush, the mavis.

"I have never seen a man fairy nor a woman fairy, but my mother saw a troop of them. She herself and the other maidens of the village were once out upon the summer sheiling. They were milking the cows, in the evening gloaming, when they observed a flock of fairies reeling and setting upon the green plain in front of the knoll.

And, oh King! but it was they the fairies themselves that had the right to the dancing, not the children of men! Bell-helmets of blue silk covered their heads, and garments of green satin covered their bodies, and sandals of yellow membrane covered their feet. Their heavy brown hair was streaming down their waist, and its luster was of the fair golden sun of summer. Their skin was as white as the swan of the wave, and their voice as melodious as the mavis of the wood, and they themselves were as beauteous of feature and as lithe of form as a picture, while their step was as light and stately and their minds as sportive as the little red hind of the hill. The damsel children of the sheiling-fold never saw sight but them, no never sight but them, never aught so beautiful."

A Note on Fairy Lore

Belief in fairies is one of the cultural features that united the traditional, preindustrial societies of Europe. In this book, I have confined myself to the fairy lore of northern Europe, which despite significant cultural differences displays a remarkable coherence as a body of belief. The English brownie, the Scottish bauchan, the Welsh bwca, the Scandinavian tomte or nisse, the German kobold — these household fairies are all recognisably the same kind of creature. Not only are they described similarly, but similar stories are told about them.

In this book, I have retold some of these stories, placing them in the particular local context in which each version was recorded. Many of these place names will be unfamiliar, but I think they are worth preserving. Sometimes the story could just as well be set anywhere; sometimes the place name and the story will intertwine. For instance the place where Little John lived in the Scottish story of "The Water Horse" (p. 63) is called to this day Dalchapple, which means Horsefield.

Throughout Europe, the existence of the fairy folk was once taken for granted. When the Irish poet W. B. Yeats, scouting for fairy lore in his native County Sligo, asked Paddy Flynn— "a little bright-eyed old man"—whether he had ever seen the fairies, the answer was a resigned, "Am I not annoyed with them?"

When these words were spoken, toward the end of the nineteenth century, it seemed the fairies, once so plentiful, were vanishing into thin air, and fairy beliefs with them. Yet here and there pockets of fairy faith have survived, and it may be that the fairies have not departed for good, but only retreated temporarily from the noise, bustle, and sophistication of our modern world.

The fairies of folk tradition are beings of magical power, who must be treated with respect. They may help human beings who please them, and harm those who offend them. They are both more majestic and more mischievous than the sentimental flower fairies of modern fancy—what Rudyard Kipling's Puck in *Puck of Pook's Hill* calls "that painty-winged, wand-waving, sugar-and-shake-your-head set of impostors."

The modern image of the fairy as an ethereal creature with butterfly wings owes more to literature than tradition. William Shakespeare's inclusion of the fairies Titania, Oberon, and Puck in *A Midsummer Night's Dream* encouraged writers to develop their own ideas of the fairies. The often ugly or frightening fairies of folklore were replaced by more delicate creatures. The eighteenth-century poet Alexander Pope, for instance, compared fairies to the sylphs and nymphs of classical times, and spoke of their "insect-wings" and "transparent bodies."

"There never was a merry world," said the seventeenth-century writer John Selden, "since the fairies left off dancing." But have they quite left off? In art and story they are dancing still. In the words of a poem such as W.B. Yeats's "The Stolen Child" we may yet hear the echo of their mesmerizing call, tempting us to leave our humdrum human world and run away to carefree fairyland:

> Come away! O, human child!
> To the woods and waters wild,
> With a fairy hand in hand,
> For the world's more full of weeping
>   than you can understand.

A Note on Fairy Paintings

Although belief in fairies stretches back into antiquity, the attempt to depict them in art is relatively recent. It began in the late eighteenth-century, with the work of visionary artists such as William Blake (1757-1827). But although Blake believed in fairies (for his account of a fairy funeral, see p. 9), his fairy paintings illustrated scenes from literature, such as "Oberon, Titania, Puck, and Fairies Dancing" (p. 81) from Shakespeare's *A Midsummer Night's Dream*.

Shakespeare's play, with its squabbling fairy king and queen, and the mischievous figure of Puck, remained a key source of inspiration for British fairy painters in what the art critic Christopher Wood has called "the golden age of fairy painting," from about 1840 to 1870.

The most famous of all the fairy painters was Richard Dadd (1817-1886). In the early 1840s he made his name with a series of fairy paintings inspired by *A Midsummer Night's Dream* and *The Tempest*. In 1843, Dadd began to suffer from delusions. Believing that his father was the devil, he stabbed him to death; he was confined to mental hospitals for the rest of his life.

Dadd's promising artistic career was over before it had truly begun. But he continued to paint, and it was in the Bethlem Royal Hospital that he produced his masterpiece "The Fairy Feller's Master-Stroke" (p. 56). This painting took nine years to complete. Dadd worked on it obsessively, filling every scrap of canvas with surreal detail. The result is a haunting picture that seems to capture a moment of fairy life with the clear-eyed intensity of one who has rubbed fairy ointment in his eye. For just this one instant, the artist's gaze can penetrate the fairy glamour.

Richard Dadd's earlier works strongly influenced a number of fairy painters, notably Sir Joseph Noël Paton (1821-1901), John George Naish (1824-1905), and John Anster Fitzgerald (1832-1906). The work of such artists referred more often to literature than to fairy folklore, but nevertheless aspects of traditional fairy belief rise to the surface. Paton's "La Belle Dame Sans Merci" (p. 99) takes its title from John Keats, but actually illustrates the famous Scottish legend of Thomas the Rhymer; John Anster Fitzgerald has given us the only known painting of a fairy funeral (p. 10).

Victorian fairy painting reached its imaginative heights in the hands of Richard Doyle (1824-1883). Doyle's work anticipates that of Arthur Rackham (1867-1939) and was in turn strongly influenced by that of the great illustrator George Cruikshank (1792-1878); Cruikshank's eerie watercolor "A Fantasy, The Fairy Ring" (p. 79) is a sketch for his frontispiece to the 1850 edition of Thomas Keightley's classic study of fairy lore, *The Fairy Mythology*.

Richard Doyle painted many charming watercolors of fairy subjects (such as "The Altar Cup in Aagerup," p. 71), but his finest contributions to fairy art were his illustrations to the book *In Fairyland* (1870). A number of Doyle's charming and playful images from this classic book appear in *The Little People*, for instance on the title page.

In Britain, many lesser-known artists produced beautiful fairy paintings in the Dadd/Doyle tradition. Elsewhere, illustrators and painters were also drawn to the subject, notably in Scandinavia, where artists such as Nils Blommer (1816-53), Ernst Josephson (1851-1910), and John Bauer (1882-1918), conjured powerful images of the fairy world.

Each of the artists whose work graces this book has enriched our vision of fairyland, a world of mystery and temptation where reality and imagination meet. While their paintings do not literally illustrate the text, they have been chosen in the hope that the art and stories might blend together to convey the magic of the fairy world.

Illustration Credits

The history of fairy paintings and illustrations is well covered in *Victorian Fairy Painting*, edited by Harriet Martineau, and in *Fairies in Victorian Art*, by Christopher Wood.

All pencil drawings are by Jacqueline Mair, and were specially commissioned for this book. Pictures by Walter Crane (1845-1915) on pp. 6, 9, 16, 48, 92, and 106 are reproduced from *Flora's Feast* (London, Cassell, 1889), and on pp. 24, 32, 64, 97, and 102 from *Flowers from Shakespeare's Garden* (London: Cassell, 1906); pictures by Richard Doyle (1824-83) on the endpapers. half-title, title, title verso, and pp. 2-3, 21, 27, 40, 43, 51 (detail), 54, 89, 109, and 110 are reproduced from *In Fairyland: A Series of Pictures of the Elf-World* (London: Longmans, Green, Reader, & Dyer, 1870).

The other color illustrations are by various artists as listed below. They are reproduced courtesy of the following institutions: frontispiece, and pp. 10, 12, 18, 23, 28, 35, 39, 44, 47, 61, 62, 66, 75, 76, 82, 90, 99, and 108, The Bridgeman Art Library; pp. 53 and 79, © copyright The British Museum; pp. 5, 37, 95, and 105, Fine Art Photographic Library; p. 85, The Folklore Society; pp. 14, 31, and 71, Sotheby's Picture Library; pp. 56 and 81, © Tate, London 2001; pp. 87 and 101, courtesy of the Trustees of the V&A.

frontispiece: Edward Robert Hughes (1851-1914) "Midsummer Eve" *The Maas Gallery, London*

5: Henry Meynell Rheam (1859-1920) "Once Upon a Time" *Private collection*

10: John Anster Fitzgerald (1832-1906) "The Fairy's Funeral" *The Maas Gallery, London*

12: Sir John Everett Millais (1829-96) "Ferdinand Lured by Ariel" *The Makins collection*

14: Paul Gustave Doré (1832-83) "Les Fées" *Private collection*

18: John George Naish (1824-1905) "Midsummer Fairies" *Christopher Wood Gallery, London*

23: Henry Meynell Rheam (1859-1920) "Queen Mab" *The Fine Art Society, London*

28: Frederick McCubbin (1855-1917) "What the Little Girl Saw in the Bush" *Private collection*

31: Eleanor Fortescue Brickdale (1871-1945" "The Introduction" *Private collection; all rights reserved*

35: Edward Reginald Frampton (1872-1923) "Fairy Land" *The Maas Gallery, London*

37: Richard Doyle (1824-83) "The Haunted Park" *Private collection*

39: Edward Robert Hughes (1851-1914) "Twilight Fantasies" *The Maas Gallery, London*

44: Arthur Rackham (1867-1939) "Dancing with the Fairies" *Private collection; © reproduced with the kind permission of his family*

47: John Bauer (1882-1918) "A Forest Troll" *Nationalmuseum, Stockholm*

53: Richard Doyle (1824-83) "Under the Dock Leaves" *The British Museum*

56: Richard Dadd (1817-86) "The Fairy Feller's Master-Stroke" *The Tate Gallery*

61: John Chamberlayne (1821-1910) "Water Sprites in a Stream" *Covent Garden Gallery, London*

62: Ernst Josephson (1851-1906) "The Water Sprite" *Nationalmuseum, Stockholm*

66: Sophie Anderson (1823-1903) "Take the Fair Face of Woman…" *The Maas Gallery, London*

71: Richard Doyle (1824-83) "The Altar Cup in Aagerup" *Private collection*

75: John Bauer (1882-1918) "Brother St. Martin and the Three Trolls" *Nationalmuseum, Stockholm*

76: Edmund Dulac (1882-1953) "Nocturnal Spires" *The Victoria & Albert Museum; all rights reserved*

79: George Cruikshank (1792-1878) "A Fantasy, the Fairy Ring" *The British Museum*

81: William Blake (1757-1827) "Oberon, Titania, and Puck, with Fairies Dancing" *The Tate Gallery*

82: John Bauer (1882-1918) "The Princess and the Trolls" *Nationalmuseum, Stockholm*

85: Henry Michael John Underhill (1855-1920) "Guleesh Disenchants the Fairy Steeds" *The Folklore Society*

87: Thomas Grieve (1799-1882) "The Palace of Theseus" *Victoria & Albert Museum*

90: Maud Tindal Atkinson (fl. 1906-37) "Ariel" *The Maas Gallery, London; all rights reserved*

95: Frederick Howard Michael (d. 1936) "Titania" *Private collection*

99: Sir Joseph Noël Paton (1821-1901) "La Belle Dame Sans Merci (The Story of Thomas Rhymer)" *Roy Mills Fine Paintings*

101: Richard Doyle (1824-83) "Wood Elves Hiding and Watching a Lady" *The Victoria & Albert Museum*

105: Charles Hutton Lear (1818-1903) "A Glimpse of the Fairies" *Private collection*

108: Nils Blommer (1816-53): "Fairies of the Meadow" *Nationalmuseum, Stockholm*

Bibliography

Arrowsmith, Nancy, and George Moorse. *A Field Guide to the Little People.* New York: Hill and Wang, and London: Macmillan, 1977.

Booss, Claire. *Scandinavian Folk and Fairy Tales.* New York: Gramercy Books, 1984.

Briggs, Katharine M. *Abbey Lubbers, Banshees & Boggarts: A Who's Who of Fairies.* London: Kestrel Books, and New York: Pantheon Books, 1979.

—— *A Dictionary of Fairies.* London: Allen Lane, 1976. Published as *An Encyclopedia of Fairies.* New York: Pantheon Books, 1976.

—— *The Anatomy of Puck.* London: Routledge and Kegan Paul, 1959.

—— *The Fairies in Tradition and Literature.* London: Routledge and Kegan Paul, and Chicago: University of Chicago Press, 1967.

—— *The Vanishing People: A Study of Traditional Fairy Beliefs.* London: B. T. Batsford, and New York: Pantheon Books, 1978.

Craigie, William A. *Scandinavian Folk-Lore.* Paisley and London: Alexander Gardner, 1896.

Curtin, Jeremiah. *Irish Tales of the Fairies and the Ghost World.* Mineola, N.Y.: Dover Publications, 2000; first published 1895 as *Tales of the Fairies and of the Ghost World.*

Gregory, Lady Augusta. *Visions and Beliefs in the West of Ireland.* Gerrards Cross, Bucks: Colin Smythe, 1970; first published 1920.

Grimm, Jacob and Wilhelm. *The German Legends of the Brothers Grimm.* Edited and translated by Donald Ward. Two volumes. Philadelphia: The Institute for the Study of Human Issues, 1981.

Hunt, Robert. *Popular Romances of the West of England.* London and New York: Benjamin Blom, 1968; reprint of the 3rd edition of 1881.

Keightley, Thomas. *The Fairy Mythology.* London: G. Bell, 1878; reprinted as *The World Guide to Gnomes, Fairies, Elves and Other Little People.* New York: Avenel Books, 1978.

Kirk, Robert. *The Secret Common-wealth & A Short Treatise of Charms and Spels.* Edited with a commentary by Stewart Sanderson. Ipswich and Cambridge: D. S. Brewer, and Totowa, N.J.: Rowman and Littlefield, 1976.

MacDougall, James. *Highland Fairy Legends.* Edited by George Calder with a new introduction by Dr. Alan Bruford. Ipswich and Cambridge: D. S. Brewer, and Totowa, N.J.: Rowman and Littlefield, 1978; first published 1910 as *Folk Tales and Fairy Lore in Gaelic and English.*

Martineau, Jane, ed. *Victorian Fairy Painting.* London: Merrell Holberton, 1997.

Narváez, Peter, ed. *The Good People: New Fairylore Essays.* Lexington: University Press of Kentucky, 1997.

Philip, Neil. *The Penguin Book of English Folktales.* Harmondsworth: Penguin Books, 1992.

—— *The Penguin Book of Scottish Folktales.* Harmondsworth: Penguin Books, 1995.

Purkiss, Diane. *Troublesome Things: A History of Fairies and Fairy Stories.* London: Allen Lane, 2000. Published as *At the Bottom of the Garden: A Dark History of Fairies, Hobgoblins, Nymphs, and Other Troublesome Things.* New York: New York University Press, 2001.

Rose, Carol. *Spirits, Fairies, Leprechauns, and Goblins: An Encyclopedia.* New York: W.W. Norton & Company, 1998.

Sikes, Wirt. *British Goblins.* East Ardsley. Yorks: EP Publishing Ltd, 1973; first published 1880.

Silver, Carol G. *Strange and Secret Peoples: Fairies and Victorian Consciousness.* New York and Oxford: Oxford University Press, 2000.

Simpson, Jacqueline. *Scandinavian Folktales.* Harmondsworth: Penguin Books, 1988.

Wentz, W. Y. Evans. *The Fairy-Faith in Celtic Countries.* Gerrards Cross, Bucks: Colin Smythe Ltd, 1977. First published 1911; reprinted Secaucus, N.J.: Carol Publishing Group, 1990.

Wood, Christopher. *Fairies in Victorian Art.* Woodbridge, Suffolk: Antique Collectors' Club, 2000.

Yeats, W. B. *Fairy and Folk Tales of Ireland.* Gerrards Cross, Bucks: Colin Smythe, 1973; a combined reprint of *Fairy and Folk Tales of the Irish Peasantry,* 1888, and *Irish Fairy Tales,* 1892.

Yolen, Jane. *The Fairies' Ring: A Book of Fairy Stories and Poems.* New York: Dutton, 1999.

A Glossary of Fairies

There are so many names for different kinds of fairy, and names for individual fairies, that it would be impossible to list them all here. Much fuller lists can be found in *An Encyclopedia of Fairies*, by Katharine Briggs, and *A Field Guide to the Little People*, by Nancy Arrowsmith and George Moorse. The words in italics indicate fairies with their own entry in this glossary. The numbers indicate page references.

Banshee 21-24
In Ireland and Scotland, a female fairy who foretells death. A banshee is often attached to a particular family, but warriors may also see her in her role as the washer by the ford. The word "banshee" means "fairy woman" in Gaelic. Banshees have long flowing hair and eyes red from weeping, and wear dark cloaks.

Bauchan 19-20, 109
A Scottish *brownie*, alternately mischievous and helpful. Pronounced "buckawn." Some bauchans can take the form of a goat, in which case they are known as *urisks*.

Bergfolk 73
The bergfolk, or mound folk, are Scandinavian *dwarfs*, who live under mounds and are renowned for their metalwork (unlike many fairies who are allergic to iron). They are sometimes referred to as *trolls*.

Boggart 17, 57, 58
An English word for a mischievous *brownie*.

Brownie 17-20, 45, 109
A farm or household fairy; in Lowland Scotland, spelled broonie. When angered, brownies can turn mischievous or nasty, but usually the brownie helps with chores in return for a bowl of milk and other simple treats. More lavish rewards, such as gifts of clothing, free the brownie from service. Brownies are said to be little men around three feet high, dressed in dull, ragged clothes. The Welsh name for a brownie is bwca.

Bucca-boo 9
A Cornish hobgoblin. Cornish fishermen used to leave a fish on the sand for the bucca, and Cornish children were threatened with the bucca as a nursery bogie or bug-a-boo.

Changeling 41-43
The fairies are said to steal human children, and leave behind a changeling. These changelings are sometimes fairy children, but more often aged fairies, or simply a piece of wood enchanted into the shape of a baby. Changelings fail to thrive. There are various methods of forcing changelings to identify themselves, after which the human baby may sometimes be recovered. The human captives may be turned into fairies, and given fairy eyesight by the application of a magic ointment.

Cold Lad 18-19, 27
The Cold Lad of Hilton is an individual English *brownie* who was said to be the spirit of a murdered stable boy.

Domovoy 21
The Slavic *brownie*. The plural is domoviye.

Dwarf 2, 43, 67, 74-75, 103
Small, stocky fairies found mainly in Germany and Switzerland, dwarfs are often associated with mining. The dwarfs of Scandinavia are known as *bergfolk*.

Elf 3, 49-50, 80-81, 94-98
Scandinavian mythology features light elves and dark elves; nowadays, the word "elf" simply means one of the *trooping fairies*. In Scotland these fairies are divided into two kinds, the Seelie Court and the Unseelie Court; "seelie" means "blessed."

Fairy 1-110, *passim*
The word "fairy" can be applied to any supernatural creature of human or semihuman kind. Fairies can be divided roughly into *trooping fairies*, who travel in groups, often with a king or queen, and *solitary fairies*, such as the *leprechaun* or the *brownie*. Because fairies are dangerous, they are often referred to by euphemistic phrases, such as the Good People, or the People of Peace, rather than directly named.

Fenoderee 45-48
Also spelled Phynnodderee. Fenoderee is an enormously strong *brownie* on the Isle of Man. He was originally one of the ferrishyn, the *trooping fairies*, but was banished and turned into a brownie because he fell in love with a human girl.

Folleti *13*
Italian wind fairies.

Giant *45*
Giants are fairy creatures as much larger than humans as most of the little people are smaller. They tend to be solitary, and their chief recreation is to engage in contests of strength with other giants.

Gnome *2*
An earth spirit. Gnomes are similar to *dwarfs, goblins,* or *knockers.*

Goblin *57*
A malicious, ugly fairy.

Green Children *93-94*
Two fairy children discovered in Suffolk, England, in the twelfth century.

Hob *2, 17*
Another name for a *brownie.* The prefix "hob" generally suggests a helpful fairy, as in *hobgoblin,* or hobthrust. Hobbit is another variant.

Hobgoblin *27, 57-58*
A shape-changing fairy, such as *Puck* or *Robin Goodfellow,* who delights in playing tricks on humans. The hobgoblin has a wicked sense of humor but is not evil like a *goblin.*

Hidden People *2-3*
The Hidden People (huldufolk) are the Scandinavian *elves,* so called because they are the children Eve hid from God.

Kelpie *2, 63-65, 109*
A Scottish water fairy, which can take the shape either of a man or a horse.

Knocker *49*
A helpful fairy, similar to a *kobold,* who lives in the Cornish tin mines. Knockers are similar to *dwarfs* in character but much smaller in size, resembling little men about the size of a child's doll.

Kobold *17, 24-27, 109*
A German *brownie.*

Korred *14, 67*
A Breton *dwarf,* similar to a Cornish *spriggan.*

Leprechaun *13, 67-70*
An Irish solitary fairy, the leprechaun is the fairy shoemaker. If a leprechaun can be caught, he will lead you to his pot of gold. Sometimes called a cluricaun.

Leshiye *13*
Russian forest fairies.

Lob *45*
Similar to *hob.* Lob-Lie-by-the-Fire is a gigantic English *brownie,* similar to the Manx *Fenoderee.*

Lutin *13, 57-58*
A mischievous French fairy, who can be like a *brownie* or like a *hobgoblin.* Lutins can change their shape into anything they like.

Massariol *13*
The Italian *brownie.*

Mermaid *2, 54-55, 59*
Mermaids and mermen are the fairies of the sea, with human bodies but fishtails instead of legs. Mermaids are said to use their beauty to lure sailors to their deaths, and mermen in both Irish and German legends are said to keep the souls of the drowned in wicker "soul cages" under the sea.

Neck *60-63*
The neck (or nök, or näck) is a Scandinavian water fairy. A neck can transform into a horse, like the Scottish *kelpie.* Necks are famous musicians.

Nisse *48, 58, 109*
The Danish *brownie.*

Oberon *110*
The name of the king of the fairies in Shakespeare's *A Midsummer Night's Dream.*

Pixy *13, 102*
The fairies of Somerset, Devon, and Cornwall, in the English West Country, are often called pixies, pigsies, or piskies. They are mischievous small creatures dressed in green, who love to lead travelers astray, like *Puck*, and take horses from stables to ride at night, like the French *lutins*.

Puck *27, 110*
Puck was originally a generic name for a kind of *hobgoblin* or *pixy* who leads travelers astray in the dark, often in the form of a *will-o'-the-wisp*, a flickering light that tempts travelers from the true path. Shakespeare's shape-changing Puck in *A Midsummer Night's Dream* is almost identical in character to the mischievous fairy *Robin Goodfellow*.

Robin Goodfellow *27*
An English *hobgoblin*, a trickster fairy, similar to *Puck*.

Selkie *2, 55*
A Scottish and Irish variant on the *mermaid*, the selkie is a seal in the water but a man or woman on the ground.

Solitary fairies *2, 13, 17-27, 48-49, 67-70*
Many fairies live alone, or are only seen singly. The solitary fairies include *brownies*, *giants*, and *leprechauns*.

Spriggan *14-17*
The spriggan is a kind of Cornish fairy, said to haunt standing stones, old ruins, and places where treasure is buried; they are very similar to the *korred* of Brittany, just across the Channel in northern France. Sometimes the spriggans seem to act as guards for the Cornish *trooping fairies*. The story of Skillywidden tells of a spriggan child taken prisoner by a human in the hope of obtaining treasure.

Thomas the Rhymer *98-100, 110*
A Scottish poet who spent seven years in fairyland with the fairy queen, who gave him the gift of prophecy, which earned him the name True Thomas. At the end of his life he returned to fairyland, to be advisor to the fairy court.

Titania *4-6, 10-11, 80-81, 94-100, 110*
The name of the fairy queen in Shakespeare's *A Midsummer Night's Dream*; another name for the fairy queen is Mab. Often she is not named at all.

Tomte *17, 48-49, 109*
The Swedish and Norwegian *brownie*.

Troll *67, 70-72, 73, 82-83*
Many Scandinavian fairies are called trolls. This term may be used to mean *elves*, *dwarfs*, or *giants*; essentially the word just means "a magical being." In Iceland and Norway trolls are large and fierce; in Denmark they are as small as *pixies* or *goblins*; in Sweden they are the same size as humans. In Shetland they are called trows. Trolls are sometimes said to be unable to go out in the sun, lest its rays turn them to stone.

Trooping fairies *4-6, 10-11, 13, 45, 53, 77, 83-89, 90-108*
Trooping fairies are often seen riding in large groups and are organized in courts, with a queen (sometimes called *Titania* or Mab) and a king (sometimes called *Oberon*). They live in fairy hills or in an underground fairyland, and can resemble human beings in size and appearance. They are called the Sidhe or Tuatha de Danann in Ireland, the Tylwyth Teg in Wales, and the ferrishyn in the Isle of Man. The Scottish trooping fairies are divided into two courts, one good and one bad, named the Seelie Court and the Unseelie Court.

Urisk *20*
A kind of *bauchan*, or Scottish *brownie*, that is half-man, half-goat.

Vila *13*
A Slav female ogre, with the gift of healing. The plural is vily.

Water fairies *2, 54-55, 59, 60-65, 109*
Fairies who live in saltwater are the *mermaids* and mermen, and the *selkies*. Many other fairies live in ponds, lakes, rivers, and streams, including the Scottish water horse, the *kelpie*, and the Scandinavian *neck*. An asrai is a kind of English freshwater mermaid.

Will-o'-the-Wisp *13, 27*
A fairy who leads travelers astray, such as *Puck*, *Robin Goodfellow*, or their continental equivalent, the hey-hey men, who mislead travelers by calling out "Hey!", as if to say, "Follow me!"

Wood fairies *7-8*
Wood elves and forest spirits are found all over Europe. The Scandinavian wood fairies are said to have hollow backs. The German *kobolds*, or household *brownies*, are said to have originally been wood fairies.